Short Shorts

Volume 1

Three One-Act Plays
by Michael Yates

Nettle Books

Published 2013 by Nettle Books

nettlebooks@hotmail.co.uk

ISBN: 978-0-9561513-3-9

Classification: Drama

Cover picture by Tracey Yates, originally used for the poster of *Sunday Afternoon Again,* performed at the Write Now One-Act Play Festival in Liverpool 2012.

How to make a drama out of life

I am very much a Yorkshire playwright. All my plays have been performed in the White Rose county; and when some of them stray over the border into Liverpool or Manchester, it feels exotic.

In 1994 I was commissioned by Wakefield Libraries to write a full-length play about the history of Pontefract to commemorate the Yorkshire town's 800th birthday. Stage drama was entirely new to me; I had previously published short stories and poems. And, as a working class child, I had been brought up in the twin cultures of TV and movies; the only time I went to "live theatre" was to see pantomime. But with *Pontefractions* – as the play came to be called – I was lucky enough to come up with a single great idea.

I was aware of falling into the slough of historical pageant, of having William the Conqueror step forward and say: "It was a sunny summer in Pontefract when I built the castle..." I couldn't abandon entirely the idea of historic figures giving testimony, but my conceit was to make it part of a trial, subject to cross-examination, and so give it dramatic effect.

The play is obviously a humorous piece. A strange craft comes down to earth and a young Pontefract couple are kidnapped. But the aliens turn out to be a sort of Celestial Old Bailey. The judge is the Archangel Michael, the prosecutor is Satan, and the Pontefract couple are the Defence. Will Pontefract go to Heaven or Hell as a judgement on its mottled moral history? The audience was the jury on each of the five nights we were performing at Pontefract Town Hall and we scored it three nights for Heaven and only two for Hell, though we cunningly fixed it on the last night to give the run a "happy ending".

Later I joined up with Helen Shay, a writer I had known a few years previous, and we decided to unite in a double bill of one-act plays. Helen had already had much success with a play called *Fit Piece*, in which a young woman joins a gym and is menaced by a sinister personal coach. In shameless deference, I had meanwhile written a play called *Life Sentence*, where the situation was reversed and a woman threatened a man. This was first performed in the upstairs room of a pub in Wakefield. But because it was such an obvious companion piece to Helen's play, we showed off their relationship to good effect in a joint production called *Body Double*. And in 2009, *Life Sentence* won an award at the Sheffield One-Act Play Festival.

During the next five years, I saw more of my one-act plays performed: *Till My Eyes Bleed*, a tale of adultery and death leavened by a few good jokes, is also in this volume.

The third one-act play in this book is *Sunday Afternoon Again*, which began life as a short story published in an anthology called *Yorkshire Mixture*; then became a radio play broadcast by Bradford Community Radio and others; and was finally turned into a stage play and selected for the 2012 Write Now Drama Festival in Liverpool.

These plays were fun to write and I trust they are fun to read. Drama should always be a pleasurable surprise. I hope you find it so.

Michael Yates 2013

Contents

Life Sentence

...is the most travelled of any of my plays. This sad/comic story of a jealous wife and her threats of violence was premiered in the upstairs room at Henry Boons, a pub in Wakefield, in 2007 as part of a double bill called *Table Dancing*, performed by the Hands-On theatre company. Cast and crew were:

The woman...Emma Wise
The Man...Carl Miller

Directed by Jim Wilson.
Running time: 30 minutes

In 2008 it was performed by the ***Act*ONE** company as part of a double bill called *Body Double* in Pontefract and at The Carriageworks theatre in Leeds. In 2009, it was accepted for the Sheffield One-Act Play Festival and the production went on to win the Stanley Arnold Trophy, with female lead Joanne Smart winning the Best Actress prize. In 2010 it was performed by the DNA company in Manchester, as part of a double bill called *Guilty*.

Characters:

The Woman: A strong, commanding, middle-aged woman wearing a trouser suit, who reveals her suppressed romanticism by peppering her speech with quotes from pop songs

The Man: A much less commanding figure, casually dressed in jeans and shirt, whose references to films show him up as a movie buff

Scene: The room of a house

Time: The Present

Furniture: One table, two chairs.

Props: A high-heeled shoe, a supermarket bag, a few other shoes, half a dozen photographs, a meat cleaver.

SCENE: THE STAGE IS BARE EXCEPT FOR A TABLE WITH TWO WOODEN CHAIRS – ONE STAGE LEFT, THE OTHER STAGE RIGHT – AND A LARGE SUPERMARKET BAG STAGE LEFT.

ENTER STAGE RIGHT, MAN RUNNING, CHASED BY BAREFOOT WOMAN CARRYING A STILETTO-HEELED SHOE IN AGGRESSIVE MANNER. HE IS CHASED ROUND THE TABLE THREE OR FOUR TIMES WITH THE WOMAN TRYING TO HIT HIM WITH THE SHOE. EVENTUALLY HE TAKES REFUGE UNDERNEATH THE TABLE.

WOMAN: (SHOUTING) Come on out! Come on out, you coward! You bastard! (BANGS SHOE ON TABLE) Come on out and take your medicine! Like a man! Like the man you never were!

SHE CIRCLES THE TABLE, BANGS IT REPEATEDLY WITH HER SHOE AND LUNGES AT HIM AS HE CONTINUES TO COWER

MAN: (POKING HIS HEAD OUT FROM UNDER THE TABLE) Look! Wait!

WOMAN: (SHOUTING) Come on out! Come on out! (HER TONE BECOMES SARCASTIC) Oh, we've found our level now, haven't we? Down on the floor, down on the ground, cringing like a dog! Well, you ain't never caught a rabbit and you ain't no friend of mine! Oh, we've found our level allright! (SHE REPEATS THE SHOE-BANGING ROUND THE TABLE) Allright then! (SHE STRAIGHTENS UP, SPEAKS MORE CALMLY) You can't stay there for ever! I won't let you. If it's a life sentence for you, it's a life sentence for me as well. And I'm not doing with that!

SHE REPEATS THE SHOE-BANGING

MAN: (POKING HIS HEAD OUT AGAIN) Look…

WOMAN: (SHOUTING) What would that mother of yours think of her precious son now? Little boy, bit of a lad, likable rogue, just like his dad, real man, he-man, man among men! Do you take this man? (GAZING AT FREE HAND AS THOUGH HOLDING DOCUMENT AND MIMICKING TONE OF DOTING MUM) And here's his school report. He was always good at games. Always good at rugby. Always good at PE! Here's a picture of him in his shorts. When he came second in cross-country. Here's one in his swimming trunks. Look, he's still wet. And that's when he grew his hair long. But it was only a phase, wasn't it? He soon grew out of that. (STARTS SHOUTING AGAIN) Come on out! Come on out!

SHE REPEATS THE SHOE-BANGING

MAN: (POKING HIS HEAD OUT AGAIN) Wait…

WOMAN: (GAZING AT HAND, SPEAKING IN DOTING MUM TONE AGAIN): And here's one of him with Heather, his cousin. Sometimes I think they were more like brother and sister, they were so close. She's an air hostess now. And here's one of him with that Janet Winslow, who was head girl when he was head boy. And here's one of him at university - no, I can't remember *her* name. They seem to be enjoying themselves, don't they? I always think it's nice for young people to go out and enjoy themselves. (STARTS SHOUTING) So come out and enjoy yourself, why don't you?

REPEATS SHOE-BANGING

MAN: (POKING HIS HEAD OUT AGAIN) Can I just… ?

WOMAN: (IN DOTING MUM TONE AGAIN) I never thought he'd get married so young. I always thought he'd want to enjoy his freedom. Oh, I'm sure you'll make him happy, dear. But he *is* very young. (BACK IN HER OWN VOICE) You're not so young now! Not so fit! Getting old, middle aged spread, losing your hair! (MORE CALMLY NOW, CLEARLY IMITATING HUSBAND) I'll be a bit late tonight, dear. Late at the office. Bit late tomorrow as well. Out for a bit on Saturday, back for tea. Out for a bit! (LAUGHS) Fitness classes, down the gym, down the bloody gym. (SHOUTING) Up the bloody Alison, more like. Up the bloody Linda and Mary and Miriam and Gillian!

SHE REPEATS SHOE-BANGING

MAN: (POKING HIS HEAD OUT AGAIN) Can't we… ?

WOMAN: (AFTER PAUSE FOR BREATH) And you thought I didn't know! The phone calls! The letters! You thought I wouldn't guess. Thought I was stupid! (SHOUTING) Well, I'm *not* stupid! (EMPHASISING EVERY WORD WITH THE CRASH OF THE SHOE ON THE TABLE) I'm -not – stu-pid! - I'm - not –stu-pid!

MAN: (POKING HIS HEAD OUT AGAIN) Can't we just talk?

WOMAN: Talk! It's a long way past talking, don't you think? Or *don't* you think? Maybe you don't think at all!

MAN: (SHEEPISHLY) I think we should talk. I really do.

WOMAN: (REPEATS SHOE-BANGING) This is talk. This is me talking for once! Fat chance I get to do the talking most of the time!

MAN: (POKING HIS HEAD OUT AGAIN) Allright. Maybe it's *my* fault. Some of it. I mean, we can't go on like this. Let me out. Think of the furniture. Let's talk. I'll listen. I promise.

WOMAN: We're not playing a game you know. It's not bloody monopoly. It's the price of love! There's not a bloody get-out-of-jail-free card.

MAN: Let's say we'll have a little talk. (WARMS TO HIS THEME) Let's say we'll just talk for, oh, I don't know, half an hour? No? OK then, 20 minutes. (LOOKS AT HIS WATCH) Tell you what. You keep the shoe.

WOMAN GOES OVER TO BAG LYING STAGE LEFT AND TAKES OUT TWO MORE SHOES

MAN: Keep all the shoes. Look, you can have mine. Honest. Here.

HE TAKES OFF HIS SHOES AND PASSES THEM OUT UNDER THE TABLE

WOMAN: (PICKING UP SHOES, PUTTING THEM IN BAG) That's a bit better. I can relate to that. Decommissioning of shoes. I can see that. I can see that might be worth responding to.

MAN: Can I come out now? I feel like The Birdman of Alcatraz. (HE COMES OUT WARILY) Honest. I don't know why you behave like this. I've never been violent, have I?

WOMAN: Only because I've never given you the chance. OK. (HER ANGER APPEARS TO SUBSIDE) There. Sit there.

INDICATES WITH SHOE THE CHAIR STAGE RIGHT. MAN PULLS IT TO CENTRE OF STAGE AND SITS ON IT. WOMAN, CARRYING BAG, PULLS CHAIR FROM STAGE LEFT OVER TO CENTRE STAGE AND SITS ON IT SO THEY ARE CLOSE TOGETHER, FACING EACH OTHER.

WOMAN: OK. OK.

SHE PUTS BAG DOWN BY HER FEET

MAN: OK. Right. Where do we start?

WOMAN: Your mother. That's a good place to start. After all, it's where you started. She's a bitch, that woman.

MAN: Yes. I agree. Well, I don't actually like the word *bitch*. I think it's demeaning to women. Let's say she's a (BEAT) strong woman. But then so are you. At least that's one thing you can thank her for. She made me grow up with a taste for strong women. (SMIRKS)

WOMAN: Taste? Did you say taste? Don't make me sound like a dry white wine, a Chardonnay or a Pinot Grigio. *That* would be demeaning.

MAN: Sorry. Anyway, you've done my mum. Summed her up. Pretty well, I thought. And that cousin of mine...

WOMAN: Heather.

MAN: And that Janet...

WOMAN: Winslow.

MAN: Right. Neither of them meant anything. It's just that my mother expected...

WOMAN: That you'd go out with girls. Of course. Girls who were safe. Non-threatening. Not like me. *I'm* threatening, aren't I? (WAVES THE SHOE AGAIN BUT HALF-HEARTEDLY) And all those girls at University...

MAN: They meant nothing!. God, they had (BEAT) no intelligence. No independence of thought...

WOMAN: Go on...

MAN: (SMIRKS AGAIN) Not like *you*. Oh no. I don't know why women like that ever want to go to University.

WOMAN: Some women only go to get a man. They go round calling you sister all the time and offering you the use of their speculum for self-knowledge sessions. But they never fooled *me*. Just there to get a man. Get him into bed. Then it's hi-ho-hi-ho, a housewife's life for me.

MAN: Hi-diddle-de-dee.

WOMAN: What?

MAN: It's hi-diddle-de-dee, a housewife's life for me.

WOMAN: Yes. That's it. That's quite well put.

MAN: Pinocchio. 1940. Only there it's an *actor's* life of course.

WOMAN: Of course. Well, you'd know a lot about acting!

MAN: Well…

WOMAN: (HER VOICE RISES AGAIN) Acting. Lying. Scheming. Betraying.

MAN: No. You've got it wrong.

WOMAN How have I got it wrong then?

MAN It's ridiculous. I mean, all those women…

WOMAN: Linda, Mary, Gillian …

MAN: (JOKILY) Hannah and her sisters! (QUICKLY GETS SERIOUS AGAIN) No. I hardly know those women. They're workmates, colleagues, we have a drink together now and again. That's all.

WOMAN: Oh, I'd like to think that. But you'll have to do better. You'll have to convince me.

MAN: Allright. That Gillian for instance. Well, it's an office, for God's sake. There are little flirtations. I mean, that's how men and women work together, isn't it?

WOMAN: I wouldn't know. *I* gave up work, remember? I gave up work before I even had a job. *You* wanted that, not *me*. You wanted a baby. (HER EYES MIST OVER) You turned the spare room into a nursery. I can see you now painting little Paddington Bears on the ceiling. I thought you were really sweet in those days. And we always used to watch Top of the Pops. You always knew who was number one in those days.

MAN: Yes. I was wrong to make you give up work. Now I can see how wrong I was. Now I can see what a bully I was. Self-awareness is only bought with pain, you know. Please forgive me.

WOMAN: Well, I believe in forgiveness, you know that. When you're a woman, you have to. (BEAT) Is that the reason you started all those affairs, then? Because we couldn't have a baby?

MAN: Honest, there are no affairs. Really. Office flirtations, that's all. It's all banter. It doesn't mean anything. You bump into each other at the coffee machine.

WOMAN: Bump into each other? I'd think more of you if you admitted it. Just came out with it. I could understand if you'd just got drunk and been tempted at the Christmas party. Just once. That would be human, that would. A couple of cherry brandies. I could understand that. It's just the dishonest, calculating way you do things.

That's what gets me. Yes, if there was one little lapse and if you were man enough to admit it, then I might forgive you. If I thought you'd told me the truth. The whole truth.

MAN: OK. Allright. Gillian.

WOMAN: Gillian? The tall dark one?

MAN: (PAUSE) Yes. That's the one. OK. Christmas two years ago.

WOMAN: (KNOWINGLY) Cherry brandy.

MAN: No. I was on Stellas. She was drinking advocaat as a matter of fact. And then it sort of happened.

WOMAN: Sort of happened how many times?

MAN: Only the once. I swear. Afterwards I was so ashamed.

WOMAN: She's very attractive.

MAN: (SHRUGS) She's OK. Not as attractive as *you*. Nowhere near.

WOMAN: You're so nice to me tonight. So full of compliments.

SHE DROPS THE SHOE, PULLS A MEAT CLEAVER OUT OF THE BAG AND WAVES IT MENACINGLY

WOMAN: So! You have it off with some tart that you don't even find attractive! And that little fact is supposed to make me feel good, is it?

MAN: (STARTS IN TERROR) What's that? What's that chopper doing?

WOMAN: What's it doing? What do choppers do? Don't worry, it's just resting. Just sitting here in my hand. And it's not a chopper. It's a meat cleaver.

MAN: I thought we were vegetarians.

WOMAN: You never know when one of these is going to come in handy.

MAN: (NOW VERY NERVOUS) Oh come on now. Be fair. We're both civilised people. We can work it out.

WOMAN: Oh I know. Life is very short and there's no time for fussing and fighting, my friend. *You* work it out. You say something to convince me I shouldn't cleave your skull like a pork chop.

MAN: (VERY NERVOUS) OK. OK. I'm thinking. Where do you want me to start this time?

WOMAN: Start with Alison. It's got an A. Let's do this thing alphabetically.

MAN: Right. What's this idea you've got about Alison?

WOMAN: Don't come the innocent with me. Alison. Your precious secretary. You've been screwing that woman for the past six months. (WAVES CLEAVER) You better not lie to me now!

MAN: OK. Yes. OK.

WOMAN: (COLLAPSING IN TEARS) How could you? How could you do such a thing? Haven't I been a good wife to you?

MAN: Yes, you have. You've been great. It was never intended as any kind of slur on you.

WOMAN: Never intended as a slur on me? You're sleeping with your fuckin secretary and you say it's no slur on me? After all I've done! Don't I look after the house? Don't I vacuum every day? Don't I pick up all your dirty underpants? Don't I wash them for you?

MAN: Yes. You do. You're very clean. I like that. I admire it in you. I like having a very clean house. And clean underpants.

WOMAN: Don't I cook for you? Don't I make all your favourite dishes? Garlic bread! God, it makes you stink! And haven't I been looking after your health all this time? Getting you off the cholesterol? Yogurt in the sponge cakes instead of cream. Margarine on your wholemeal.

MAN: Yes. Yes. I eat well. Like a king. Like a very *healthy* king.

WOMAN: Is it bed then? Haven't I always tried…?

MAN: (QUICKLY) Always.

WOMAN: But some of those things (BEAT) well, no woman would do things like that! Not like in those pictures you brought home. I don't know where you get pictures like that. I don't know what woman would do such things. I don't. I won't!

MAN: No. I can see that.

WOMAN: (LEAPING TO HER FEET, WAVING CLEAVER): That Alison! She does, doesn't she? She does it all! She doesn't care what she does! I should've known. I suppose she doesn't mind that thing with the Alsatian?

MAN: No. We've never done the thing with the Alsatian. Alison is very strong on animal rights.

WOMAN: It's nice to know she's got *some* principles. (ANGER SUBSIDES A LITTLE) Oh why? Why did you do it? Is she more beautiful than I am then? Is that it?

MAN: No. Absolutely not. You're far more beautiful than Alison. Any day. You're a star. You're my Julia Roberts, you are. You're my Ingrid Bergman. Really.

WOMAN: Why then? Why did you do it?

MAN: (QUICKLY) I don't know. She means nothing to me.

WOMAN: Oh, I see. Because she means nothing to you, it's not supposed to bother me. That is so insulting! First you tell me you have it off with some tart at the Christmas party that you don't even fancy! Now you say you took up with a woman who means nothing to you. If *she* means nothing to you, what do I mean to you? Hey? Answer me that. Because if she means nothing, I must mean less than nothing! Is that it?

MAN: No, no. That's wrong. You mean everything to me. (BEAT) Stress. That's it.

Work. Overwork. She worked on me. Yes. Oh, she's a nasty piece of work. Now I think about it. She got to me. At a vulnerable time. The chief wanted all those end-of-year reports and I needed to work late. Tables of figures, reams of paper…

WOMAN: I can imagine the scene. The muted throb of the laser printer…

MAN: But I didn't think of it like that. I just thought (BEAT) oh, I don't know what I thought.

WOMAN: You thought you could get away with it!

MAN Look, I thought you'd never find out. I never meant to hurt you. Honest. I really didn't.

WOMAN: You expect me to forgive you now? You expect me to agree a new start? Because it was just one of those things? A trip to the moon on gossamer wings? Because it didn't mean anything?

MAN: But it didn't. It was (BEAT) well, I don't know how to describe it exactly…

WOMAN: Well, *I* do! *I* know how to describe it! Wicked, that's what *I'd* call it! There. That's a good start, don't you think? And selfish. And what else would I call it? Let's see. Deceitful, that's another good word.

MAN: Yes. Yes. Selfish. Wicked. Deceitful. Yes, every one of those!

WOMAN: But those are *my* words. All you're doing is repeating what I say!

MAN: (ALMOST HYSTERICAL NOW) Because I'm agreeing with you! Don't you see? The scales have fallen from my eyes at last!

WOMAN: And you've not even apologised. You've not even said you're sorry.

MAN: (DESPERATE) Yes, I did. Didn't I? I'm sure I did. Anyway, I'm saying it now. Sorry! Sorry! Sorry!

WOMAN: You don't even know the meaning of the word.

MAN: Yes I do. I mean, I can't quote you exactly what's in the dictionary, not with all the derivations. But… (SPEEDS UP AS HE SEES HER BRANDISHING THE CLEAVER CLOSER TO HIS FACE) but of course I know what it means. It means: Apologies. Distress. Regret. Please forgive. Stuff like that. That's what sorry means.

WOMAN: You could at least say it as if you meant it.

MAN: (TAKING A DEEP BREATH) I'm sorry. Honestly. I don't know how I can express how sorry I am. But I *am* sorry. I mean, words are meaningless to convey the sorrow, the regret, the…

WOMAN: Distress.

MAN: .. distress. Words like that. Words I can't remember right now. Not all of them. But they're all here (POINTS) in my heart.

WOMAN: In your heart. I like that. I only wish I could believe it. I can't see into your heart. Nobody can.

MAN: Please!

WOMAN: You can't see into *my* heart either. What's hidden in our hearts is a secret, unfathomable. (PAUSE) Open your shirt.

MAN: What?

WOMAN: I said: Open your shirt. Just a little bit. Go on. I hope you're not going all shy on me.

HE UNBUTTONS HIS SHIRT, PULLS IT OPEN WITH BOTH HANDS

MAN: What are you going to do?

WOMAN: Well, I'm not going to stare at your nipples. (PAUSE) That was a joke.

MAN: (WITH FORCED LAUGH) Yes. It was a good one.

WOMAN: It shows my mood might be lightening again. (SHE SHOVES HER FREE HAND INTO HIS SHIRT) There.

MAN: There what?

WOMAN: I can feel your heart beat. It's beating very fast. Heartbeat, why do you flip when my baby touches me? Do you think that means you've been lying? Like a lie detector test?

MAN: No. No. Not at all.

WOMAN: What does it mean then?

MAN: It means I'm scared.

WOMAN: Well. Scared. (PAUSE) That's what you *should* be. Scared.

MAN: And I am.

WOMAN: Go on then. Make me.

MAN: Make you *what*?

WOMAN: Make me believe you're sorry. Using your skill and judgement. Using your own words. It's only words, but words are all you have to steal my heart away. Come on. I'm waiting.

SHE REMOVES HER HAND FROM HIS SHIRT

WOMAN: Go on. Convince me. You always did have charm. You always were persuasive. How do you think you got me in the first place? He's a charmer, I thought. He could charm the birds off the trees. And you could, couldn't you? And you're still doing it. (SHOUTS) You're still doing it, you bag of shit! Come on!

SHE SITS DOWN AGAIN

WOMAN: Now I'm sitting comfortably. (WAVES CLEAVER AGAIN) Come on! Tell me you're sorry. Make me believe it!

MAN: (STILL HOLDING HIS SHIRT FRONT OPEN) I've never felt so sorry in all my life. I've never felt so…

WOMAN: Anguished?

MAN: Yes. Anguished. It's as though I've plummeted head first into (BEAT) a boiling ocean.

WOMAN: You mean boiling like a bit choppy on the surface? Or boiling as in boiling an egg?

MAN: Er (PAUSE) A bit of both. So when I plummet into this ocean…

WOMAN: (EAGERLY) Yes?

MAN: On the one hand I'm drowning. On the other hand I'm scalded to death.

WOMAN: Both at the same time.

MAN: Yes. Simultaneously.

WOMAN: Sounds like hell.

MAN: That's what it is. It's hell.

WOMAN: It's where you belong.

MAN: Yes. It's where I belong.

WOMAN: It's what you deserve.

MAN: Yes, it's what I deserve.

WOMAN: But maybe I'll forgive you.

MAN: Please!

WOMAN: I'm going to put this (INDICATES CLEAVER) back in the bag. (SHE DOES SO)

MAN: Thanks.

WOMAN: But I'm keeping the bag within reach. (SHE PUTS IT ON HER LAP) Still, you must feel a lot happier now. Now you know I'm not going to chop off your cock. Not right away.

MAN: Oh yes. I *am* happier.

WOMAN: But don't get *too* happy.

MAN: No, no, I'm trying not to.

WOMAN: Because it's here at hand. It can still come out of the bag. *I'm* holding the bag.

MAN: I know. I can see.

WOMAN: So don't try any tricks.

MAN: No.

WOMAN: Not like some hero in those films you're always watching. Not like…

MAN: Er (BEAT) Indiana Jones? James Bond?

WOMAN: James Bond. He's not real, you see. He's only in films. He's an actor, that's all. But *this* is real. *You're* real. *I'm* real. *Alison* is bloody real. And the meat cleaver, that's real too.

MAN: I understand.

WOMAN: Because James Bond or some other film hero …

MAN: Atticus Finch.

WOMAN: Atticus Finch?

MAN: He's the lawyer in *To Kill a Mockingbird*. He's actually my number one hero. It's my favourite film.

WOMAN: But he's not a man of action. Not like James Bond.

MAN: No. Well, that's true. He's not. More an intellectual. Not a man of action at all.

WOMAN: No, he isn't. And neither are *you*. Just remember that. Oh, I used to *think* you were. I used to think you were tough and brave and someone to cling to. I hoped you'd turn out to be someone to watch over me. Like…

MAN: James Bond.

WOMAN: It's just that you might think you could get one over on me. Even now. James Bond might think he could jump out of that chair and snatch this bag out of my hands and throw me to the ground and overpower me with his brute strength…

MAN: (CONSIDERING) Hmmmm.

WOMAN: And maybe James Bond *could*. But you couldn't. Could you?

MAN: No.

WOMAN: Because you're not a man of action, are you?

MAN: No.

SHE SUDDENLY LEAPS TO HER FEET AGAIN AND PULLS MEAT CLEAVER OUT OF BAG

WOMAN: Except the kind of action you and Alison have been getting up to!

MAN: (ABSOLUTELY TERRIFIED) Aaaaghhh!!

HE NEARLY FALLS OFF HIS CHAIR BUT SHE GRABS IT WITH HER FREE HAND AND STEADIES HIM

WOMAN: (DRAWING BACK) And you can do your shirt up now.

MAN: (HIS HANDS ARE STILL HOLDING THE SHIRT OPEN) Right. OK. Thanks.

HE BUTTONS HIS SHIRT WITH SHAKY HANDS

WOMAN: I won't be rummaging in there again. Not just now. Because now I want to hear about the rest. In detail. Names, places, how good they all were. Why you didn't think *I* was better. Let's start with Linda.

MAN: (CONFUSED) Linda?

WOMAN: Don't tell me we've forgotten Linda. The one with the hair extensions. Was she another one who didn't mean anything to you?

MAN: Oh no.

WOMAN: (MENACINGLY) No?

MAN: I mean yes. She never meant a thing.

WOMAN: Nor Mary and Miriam and Gillian and Caroline and…

MAN: (MOOD SUDDENLY CHANGES) Look. Hang on. I don't think I ever had any of those women. In fact, I'm sure I never did. Not even Gillian. I know I *said* I did. But I think we're going a bit too far now. We're over-reaching ourselves. Look at it this way: where's my (TICKS OFF A FINGER) motivation? Hey? Answer me that. Where's my (TICKS OFF ANOTHER FINGER) opportunity? No, I'd never have the time. Not with *my* work schedule. And I'd be too tired. Don't forget: I've studied your husband. And the way I read his character…

WOMAN: The way you what? *I'm* the one who knows his character. *I* know him! Not you! *You* don't know him!

MAN: I know him from what you've told me. The secretary… Yes. I can see that. That's very plausible.

WOMAN: (CRESTFALLEN) You can? Oh God. Plausible? Is it really?

MAN: Oh yes. Bosses and secretaries. Work together. Think like a team. It happens. But not all those others. Believe me. It's a professional opinion. I'm an actor, after all. I know about character.

HE LOOKS AT HIS WATCH, HIS WHOLE MANNER HAS CHANGED NOW, HE IS SUDDENLY CONFIDENT

MAN: Anyway, time is up. (PAUSE) The cleaver, by the way, was brilliant. Shoes have sole but a cleaver has menace, that's what I say. It had me really scared. Now and again. Nice one.

HE GETS UP AND STRETCHES, LOOKS AROUND, SMILES, POINTS AT HIS STOCKINGED FEET

WOMAN: (DEFLATED): Oh yes. Right. Here.

SHE PICKS UP THE BAG, PUTS THE CLEAVER BACK INSIDE AND TAKES OUT HIS SHOES

MAN: Thanks

HE SITS DOWN, PUTS HIS SHOES BACK ON, GETS TO HIS FEET

WOMAN: You'll want your money now. It's still fifty, is it?

SHE TAKES SOME NOTES OUT OF THE BAG, COUNTS THEM OUT, HANDS THEM OVER WITHOUT LOOKING AT HIM. HE TAKES THEM, ALSO COUNTS THEM, PUTS THEM AWAY.

MAN: (SMILES) Right. Perfect. Thanks a lot. Same time next week? Is that OK?

WOMAN: (STILL NOT LOOKING AT HIM) Yes. Fine. (PAUSE) You're right. You better go now. My husband's due back in half an hour. And we don't want him to know about our little arrangement, do we? (FINALLY LOOKS HIM IN THE FACE) It's getting so he always works late on Wednesdays. Well, you *know* that. Like every other day of the week.

MAN: (HE NODS) Next week then. Well, thanks again.

HE WALKS OFF JAUNTILY, EXITS STAGE RIGHT SHE SITS ON THE EDGE OF THE TABLE WATCHING AFTER HIM, THEN CALLS OUT

WOMAN: No. No. (PAUSE) I'm the one who should be thanking you. (SHE LAUGHS AND WAVES) So! Break a leg!

SHE TURNS AWAY, HER HEAD SLUMPS, THEN AFTER A WHILE SHE GETS UP, REARRANGES THE CHAIRS UNDER THE TABLE, PICKS UP THE SUPERMARKET BAG AND WALKS DEJECTEDLY AND SLOWLY OFF STAGE RIGHT.

LIGHTS DIM

END

Till My Eyes Bleed

...is a tale of loyalty and betrayal, friendship and sex, all being exposed at a wake held by nerdy Mel for his elegant friend Adrian. The play was premiered in 2009 at Henry Boons in Wakefield, as part of a double bill called *Money Double*, performed by the ***Act*ONE** company, which moved on to The Carriageworks theatre in Leeds. Cast and crew:

Mel...David Brookmyre
Adrian...Richard Dipple
Beatrice..Rachel Vernelle
Crystal/Amy..Sal Fulcher
Terry/Announcer......................................Colin Lewisohn

Directed by Colin Lewisohn
Running time: 60 minutes

The same year, the play was performed as a stand-alone piece at the Ilkley Literature Festival fringe.

Characters:

Mel, early 40s and always looks it, though appears in flashback as a schoolboy. He is likable, educated, but nerdy and always misses the point. He generally wears tee-shirt and casual trousers (never jeans).

Adrian, also early 40s, also flashbacks as a schoolboy, but is tall, elegant, intelligent, attractive. Mostly wears a full-length stylish leather coat, except in school sports scene, where he wears vest and shorts, and final scene with Amy, Mel and Beatrice when he affects sweaters and jeans.

Beatrice, Mel's wife, also early 40s, very attractive, smartly dressed, a bit hard, very worldly.

Crystal and **Amy**, Adrian's successive girlfriends, beautiful, mid-twenties, played by the same actress, but with very different appearances (eg in long blonde wig as Crystal, in short dark hair as Amy)

Terry, a male member of the audience, middle-aged.

Voice on station tannoy.

Time: The Gordon Brown era.

Scenes: A London railway station; and school grounds, houses and gardens in Yorkshire.

Furniture: A bench that can double as a sofa with a throw over it. Two chairs that can double as living room or bar chairs with throws. A coffee table that can double as a bar table.

Props: Various bottles and glasses, plates and cutlery.

MUSIC: YOU KNOW I'M NO GOOD BY AMY WINEHOUSE. ENTER MEL, STAGE RIGHT, WITH A TUMBLER IN ONE HAND, A MICROPHONE IN THE OTHER. HE PUTS HIS DRINK ON THE TABLE AND PULLS TABLE AND CHAIR CENTRE STAGE. HE SCANS THE AUDIENCE, THEN SITS DOWN ON THE CHAIR. MUSIC CEASES.

MEL: (WAVING TO VARIOUS SECTIONS OF THE AUDIENCE IN TURN) Eyup! Good to see you. (PAUSE) It's good music, isn't it? But we're not here for the music. (BEAT) No. I want to thank you all for coming tonight. Well worth hiring the theatre. Even in these credit crunch times.(BEAT) Now, I think I know most of you. (GAZES OUT) Hello Terry. (WAVES) Good to see you, mate. You got a drink at the bar OK? You're not still banned after last time, are you? (CONTINUES TO GAZE AROUND) Hello there, Blanche. You're looking lovely tonight, my girl. That diet's worked wonders. I mean, keep it up. Life's to be lived.(SMILES, DOES A THUMBS-UP) Unless you're dead, of course (BEAT). Which brings me to the subject of our little get-together. Very sad subject. But I don't mean that we *should* be sad. No. We're here to be happy. (RAISES HIS FISTS IN MOCK SALUTE) Happy and sad. If you can be those two things at the same time. Which I always think you can.

TERRY (FROM THE AUDIENCE) Get on with it, Mel!

MEL: (LAUGHS) Right, Terry. Ok. (TAKES DEEP BREATH) I think it's important that we do this, that we celebrate the life of our good mate Adrian Merchant, departed this world, aged

42. (BEAT) You know, Adie's death was only a very small part of his life. The only reason it's uppermost in our minds is that it's the most recent memory we have of him. But it's his *life* we're here to celebrate. So. I want us all to have a good time.(PAUSE) God, I can hear him now. No long faces, mate, he'd say. And that's what I said to Beatrice, my good lady wife, because she's not the sort for parties really. (BEAT) Yes. Adie was quite a character. Wit. Raconteur. A bit of a ladies' man. Or so I understand from certain members of the fair sex. (LAUGHS) And what's wrong with that? Cheers, Adie. (LOOKS INTO THE AIR, PICKS UP HIS GLASS, RAISES IT, DRINKS FROM IT, PUTS IT DOWN) Adie liked his drink, of course. But a man's religion is his own business. And it's not just that Adie was a clever, artistic, wonderfully talented person. He was also a great friend. We've all got stories to tell about his generosity. (HE GETS UP, WALKS TO FRONT OF STAGE, AS LIGHTS DIM TO SINGLE SPOT) To me, Adrian was a symbol of a special time when we all had our dreams. Oh, those days are not so long ago. And I'll tell you this: they'll come back again! (CHEER FROM THE AUDIENCE) But there was one scary thing about Adrian of course: just every once in a while, when you didn't think he was going to do it after all, or when you'd got a little bit merry yourself, he'd just keel over and lie on the floor or wherever. And somebody would say: "Adie's had a drop too much" or "Too many bevvies, old son". Then that somebody and one or two others – we've all done this, haven't we ? – would carry him to the nearest bed. And in the morning, he'd be right as rain, and he'd always say something clever, something you'd always remember…

ADRIAN: (A DISEMBODIED VOICE FROM THE DARKNESS) I feel like the ground broke my fall.

LIGHTS GO UP AT THE BACK. ADRIAN IS STANDING CENTRE STAGE, SCRATCHING HIS HEAD, YAWNING, STRETCHING, TAKING STOCK

ADRIAN: (IN EXAGGERATED THEATRICAL TONES) Mel, Mel, Mel! Is it the middle of the night? Is it really? Have I slept the clock round? You shouldn't have let me.

MEL: (PUTTING DOWN MIKE AND GLASS AND RUSHING OVER OBSEQUIOUSLY) No, no. It's morning. I just haven't opened the curtains yet. Honest. Here! Look!

MEL RUSHES STAGE RIGHT, MAKES MOTIONS WITH HIS ARMS TO INDICATE OPENING CURTAINS, WE HEAR THE SWISH AND LIGHT POURS IN

MEL: There. I wouldn't let you miss out on the sunshine, Adie.

ADRIAN: (SUDDENLY RUBBING HIS EYES FRANTICALLY AS IF IN PAIN) Have a heart, young Mel! Have a heart, you cock-sucking dwarf!

MEL: (DIRECT TO AUDIENCE) Adie always did have a way with words. But he was only being friendly. Really.

ADRIAN: Can't you see I'm a tiny bit under the weather? What sort of rotgut have you been feeding me?

MEL: (TO ADRIAN) Just the regular stuff, Adie. OK, it's not the dearest in the supermarket. But it's not that Netto crap either. (TO AUDIENCE) I was only a student after all. I was living on my government loan in those days. My university life was very bohemian as a matter of fact. Just because I was reading company law didn't mean I'd sold out to the industrial military complex. I know Adie thought he had more street cred than me just because he went to art school and wore long overcoats. (HE RUSHES STAGE BACK RIGHT) Here, it is a bit on the bright side, isn't it?

HE MAKES DESPERATE CURTAIN-CLOSING MOTIONS. WE HEAR THE SWISH ONCE AGAIN AND THE SEMI-DARKNESS RETURNS

ADRIAN: (SCATHINGLY) Not the Netto, eh? Not the Netto in the ghetto. Well, that's something for which to be vaguely thankful. I suppose Sainsbury's Glen Campbell or Asda's Infamous Grouse is at least one step in the right direction. (BEAT) God, I've run out of cigarettes. (SEARCHING IN POCKETS) You don't.. ? No, of course not. (HE SLOUCHES OVER TO THE TABLE, PICKS UP THE GLASS AND EYES IT SUSPICIOUSLY) Is this your breakfast, young Mel?

MEL: Oh no. I'm strictly a black coffee man in the mornings, Ade. Coffee and cornflakes.

ADRIAN: Black coffee sounds excellent. (BEAT) You don't have a drop of that Asda stuff left, do you? Just to take the sting out of the caffeine.

MEL: I might have a drop under the stairs. I'll go and look.

ADRIAN: You mean next to the gas meter?

MEL: Yeah, that's right.

ADRIAN: Ah. No, I'm afraid you don't. Not any more. Don't you remember, young person? I stumbled on a bottle or two at the end of the night. Quite a surprise to find it there, but I suppose if you don't have a cellar…

MEL: It's because I've joined a Christmas club, you see. So I get some of my drink in early and store it…

ADRIAN: Christmas clubs are rather working class, aren't they? (BEAT) But you don't have to apologise. Surely we've been friends long enough?

MEL: (TO AUDIENCE) It was true. We'd been friends ever since school. We met in cross country running.

ADRIAN THROWS OFF HIS GREATCOAT TO REVEAL SHORTS AND VEST. HE JOINS MEL AT FRONT OF STAGE. MEL ALSO STRIPS OFF TO VEST AND SHORTS. THE LIGHTS GO UP.

ADRIAN: (RUNNING ON SPOT) There can't be anything in life more boring than cross-country running.

MEL: (RUNNING ON SPOT, PANTING) Oh, do you think so? I think it's quite good really. Better than running round the gym.

ADRIAN: Better than running round the gym. Yes, you certainly have a point there, young'un.

MEL: (TO THE AUDIENCE) He was only one year older than me.

ADRIAN: I suppose you're very much into nature, aren't you, young... What is it you call yourself?

MEL: Simmons. Melvin Simmons.

ADRIAN: Young Simmons. Well, I'm Adrian Merchant.

MEL: Yes, I know! (TO AUDIENCE) Of course, I knew. Adrian Merchant. Editor of the lower school newspaper. Captain of the under-13s rugby team. Winner of the Wesley St John prize for the best annual essay on sportsmanhip.

ADRIAN: I suppose, being the outdoor type, you'll be one of those lads who like birds and flowers and trees, won't you? Want to be a mountain climber when you leave school, eh?

MEL: Oh no, I want to go into business. Like my dad.

ADRIAN: What's he do exactly?

MEL: Well, not a lot right now. (PAUSE) Actually, he's dead.

ADRIAN: Oh. (BEAT) Poor boy. Orphan of the storm.

MEL: It's only because of the insurance that I was able to come to St Wystan's.

ADRIAN: Well then, saved from a bog-standard comprehensive. God does exist after all.

MEL: What does *your* dad do?

ADRIAN: At the moment he's doing three years for fraudulent conversion. So I'm a bit of an orphan too.

MEL: Oh. I'm sorry.(BEAT) And what do *you* want to do? When you leave school?

ADRIAN: Write the great novel. Or be the Poet Laureate. Or paint. Politics maybe. (BEAT) And always be rich and beautiful. (BEAT) But look. Enough of this profound philosophical stuff, young reprobate. You can do me a bit of a favour...

HE STOPS RUNNING, PUTS HIS HAND DOWN HIS SHORTS AND PULLS OUT A PACKET OF MARLBOROUGHS

ADRIAN: Look, if I go behind that tree, I can have a quick drag on my Marlboroughs and you can keep watch. (HE PULLS A CIGARETTE OUT OF PACKET) You just make sure Old Spooner doesn't catch me at it.

MEL: (TO THE AUDIENCE) Old Spooner was the head of sixth. (HE STOPS RUNNING BUT CONTINUES PANTING) He liked to run behind the boys and keep watch. (TO ADRIAN) What'll you give me if I do? (TO THE AUDIENCE) I'm not a mug. I wasn't going to get into trouble with Old Spooner. Not unless I got something out of it. And there was no point Adie offering me a cigarette because I didn't smoke. (TO ADRIAN) I don't smoke, you know. (TO THE AUDIENCE) Actually, I'm 40 years old now and I've never smoked at all. I think it's stupid to take risks with your health. I'm lucky I'm not a smoker by nature. Especially in this day and age when they're so bloody expensive. (TO ADRIAN) So what'll you give me if I do?

ADRIAN: (THINKS FOR A MOMENT) I will give you my friendship for life. And if I should ever betray you, let you down in any way, which God forbid…

MEL: Yes?

ADRIAN: Then I shall kill myself.

LIGHTS GO DOWN. EXIT ADRIAN. SPOT ON MEL. HE PUTS ON TOP CLOTHES AGAIN

MEL: (TO AUDIENCE) And that was that. Friends for life. That's something you have to take seriously. So every time we did cross-country running I'd look out for Old Spooner and Adie would have his ciggy. The trouble was we'd waste a lot of time and I'd always end up last. But Adie was a natural. He could go from nought to 60 in two seconds flat. The smoking didn't seem to damage his health at all. So he always made the cross-country team anyway and I never did. Which I thought wasn't fair. I mean, the cross-country team got to go on runs all over Yorkshire and sometimes people came to watch. Girls, actually. Girls came to watch. But Adie said:

ADRIAN: (DISEMBODIED VOICE) You wouldn't like it, young Mel. It's boring. All those birds and flowers and trees. You wouldn't like it at all. We know you're not a mountain-climber.

LIGHTS GO DOWN. SOUNDS OF RAILWAY ENGINES AND CROWDS.

TANNOY: The 13.05 to Leeds will depart from platform four, calling at Peterborough, Grantham, Newark Northgate, Doncaster, Wakefield Westgate and Leeds. Platform four for the 13.05 to Leeds.

LIGHTS GO ON AT THE FRONT OF STAGE. MEL IS HURRYING ACROSS FROM STAGE RIGHT WEARING A GREY WINTER OVERCOAT WITH MATCHING SCARF AND CARRYING BLACK BRIEFCASE. ADRIAN, DRESSED IN HIS TRADEMARK OVERCOAT, IS STROLLING ACROSS FROM STAGE LEFT. THEY NEARLY COLLIDE.

ADRIAN: Can't you look..?

MEL: (SIMULTANEOUSLY) I say… Steady on!

THEY SUDDENLY RECOGNISE EACH OTHER

ADRIAN: Young Simmons! As I live and breathe!

MEL: Adie! It's Adie!

ADRIAN: My God, you young streak of vomit, it's been years!

MEL: (TO AUDIENCE) And it was true. It had been years and years and years. We'd not seen each other for.. well, years. I felt so guilty! All I could say was: well! (TO ADRIAN) Well!

ADRIAN: Well, well, this calls for a celebration. Fortunately, the station hostelry is here at hand!

MEL: (CAUGHT OUT) Agh!

ADRIAN: Agh?

MEL: What?

ADRIAN: You said Agh!

MEL: Yes. Agh! I mean, Agh! I'd very much like to but my train is about to leave. Well (LOOKS AT WATCH) in three minutes.

ADRIAN: Oh that's a shame. Which train is it?

MEL: Leeds.

ADRIAN: Still in… ?

MEL: Leeds.

ADRIAN: ...the provinces.

MEL: Yes. You..?

ADRIAN: Oh I live *here*, voodoo child. In London. The smoke. The Big Avocado as I like to call it. Hub of the known universe. Still, Leeds was always very (BEAT) nice.

MEL: Yes.

ADRIAN: A quickie perhaps? Surely? One for the rail?

MEL: Well…

ADRIAN: Those trains to Leeds are extremely frequent. So I'm given to understand. Probably more frequent than is strictly necessary.

MEL: (TO AUDIENCE) And that was it. I couldn't just bugger off home, could I? Not with the trains being so frequent. (TO ADRIAN) OK. What'll you have?

THE LIGHTS GO DOWN AT FRONT OF STAGE AND UP AT THE BACK, REVEALING A BAR TABLE WITH TWO BAR CHAIRS AND WHISKY GLASSES ON THE TABLE. MEL PUTS HIS CASE ON THE FLOOR, HE AND ADRIAN SIT DOWN AND START DRINKING.

ADRIAN: I'm awfully sorry about the train thing. I really am. Usually they're very frequent. Take my word. But now I think about it, I believe there has been some work on the line. A wood pigeon flew into an overhead cable. Something like that. That probably accounts for it. (HE LIGHTS A CIGARETTE)

MEL: That's Ok. Really. Two and a half hours isn't that long.

ADRIAN: Attaboy! (HE PUNCHES MEL ON THE ARM) Well, my young artichoke, you certainly look every inch the successful.. what is it? Businessman?

MEL: Sort of. I'm a legal adviser in intellectual property.

ADRIAN: You mean flats for students?

MEL: No. No. You see it's all about copyright and merchandising rights and… (HE TWIGS) Oh. Right. Yes. That's quite funny. But it is very interesting. Well, it *can* be.

ADRIAN: I'm sure it can. And rewarding in other ways...

MEL: It's not just the money.

ADRIAN: Oh no.

MEL: Though there's plenty of that. Intellectual property just grows and grows. It's practically the only thing that does grow in our cyberspace culture. Apart from *actual* property, of course. What my American friends call real estate. That'll always go up, whatever the economic situation.

ADRIAN: Of course.

MEL: Since the EC laws extending the period of copyright and asserting the moral right of the artist and/or licensee… (CATCHES HIMSELF) But no, it's not just the money. I mean, when you're dealing with people like Chris Martin and Amy Winehouse...

ADRIAN: You deal with Chris and Amy? That's fascinating. (BEAT) They've never mentioned you.

MEL: Er.. no. I mainly deal with Safeways and Kwikfit. (BEAT) But I liked that joke about flats for students. Yes, I'll have to tell Beatrice that one.

ADRIAN: Beatrice?

MEL: (TO AUDIENCE) My wife. (TO ADRIAN) My wife actually.

ADRIAN: My God! You're married! Young Melvin is married. I can't believe it! How on earth did that happen? Are you both in intellectual property? That would be quite a coincidence.

MEL: Not quite. She's in human resources. But it's on the legal side.

ADRIAN: Not *illegal* human resources then? Not body parts on the black market?

MEL IS JUST ABOUT TO RESPOND WHEN HE REALISES HE IS BEING KIDDED AND GRINS AWKWARDLY

ADRIAN: You two must have a lot to talk about.

MEL: (TO AUDIENCE) So I told him all about it. Told him about Beatrice and me.

THE LIGHTS GO DOWN AT THE BACK OF THE STAGE AND UP FRONT LEFT ON A SETTEE. MEL MOVES FRONT STAGE LEFT. BEATRICE IS SITTING ON THE SETTEE READING MARIE CLAIRE. MEL TAKES OFF HIS OVERCOAT, DRAPES IT ACROSS HIS ARM AND STANDS GAZING ACROSS AT HER.

MEL: (TO BEATRICE) I couldn't help noticing...

BEATRICE: (LOOKING UP FROM HER MAGAZINE) Noticing?

MEL: You. You were in the seminar. Management, Law and the Post-Industrial Economy. Part 2.

BEATRICE: I didn't see *you*.

MEL: I was at the back. I always prefer to sit at the back. You get the chance to look around, you get a good view.

BEATRICE: You got a good view of *me*, did you?

MEL: Aaagh. Well, I don't mean I was particularly looking at you...

BEATRICE: (AMUSED) You were just looking at the women in general?

MEL: Oh no, I'm not the sort of man who looks at women. Well, I *do* look at women. I mean, I'm not gay or anything. No, I do look at women. Quite a bit of the time. No, what I mean is...

BEATRICE: ...you weren't particularly interested in me.

MEL: Yes. No. I mean I did find you...

BEATRICE: Attractive?

MEL: (EMBARRASSED) Interesting.

BEATRICE: Not attractive then.

MEL: Er.. yes. Yes. Attractive. I was just sort of groping for the word.

BEATRICE: I suppose groping for words is about all the groping you ever get to do.

LIGHTS GO OFF OVER THE CHAIRS. MEL WALKS TO CENTRE STAGE FRONT. SPOTLIGHT.

MEL: (TO AUDIENCE) So that was it. We just clicked. She was the one who invited *me* out. We went to The Nip in the Bud, that Japanese vegetarian restaurant in Boar Lane. Well, actually it's closed down since then. It's a wine bar now. It's called Dregs. Oh no, wait. It closed down a second time. It's now an Oxfam shop. Anyway (BEAT) afterwards, after the very first time we went out, we went back to her *en suite* room at the Cosy Cottage Hotel. By the morning we were pretty much a couple. She told me she'd had this lengthy relationship with a married man but it came to an end when his wife got pregnant again.

BEATRICE: (JOINING MEL IN THE SPOTLIGHT AND TAKING HIS HAND) I just made up my mind about you. In the first half hour. I'm the wrong side of 35 and a girl's got to take her chances as they come.

THEY KISS

MEL: (TO AUDIENCE) It was love at first sight.

SPOTS GO OUT. LIGHTS COME UP ON ADRIAN STILL SITTING AT THE BAR TABLE AT THE BACK OF THE STAGE

ADRIAN: (CALLING INTO THE DARKNESS) If they've run out of Tomatin, it'll have to be

Johnnie Walker. Beggars can't be choosers, young arsehole.

MEL COMES OUT OF THE DARKNESS WITH THE DRINKS. HE IS AGAIN WEARING HIS OVERCOAT. HE PUTS THE GLASSES ON THE TABLE AND SITS DOWN

ADRIAN: This last girl..

MEL: Samantha.

ADRIAN: No. Alicia.

MEL: The blonde with the.. (GESTURES TO INDICATE LARGE BREASTS)

ADRIAN: No, that was Kathy.

MEL: Right.

ADRIAN: No. Alicia is the one works in PR. The trouble was…

MEL: Was..?

ADRIAN: (NOW SLURRING HIS WORDS) ...too good for me. Just too bloody good for me. They're all too good for me. I can't live up to their standards.

MEL: Right.

ADRIAN: Can't do it.

MEL: Right.

ADRIAN: Women.

MEL: Right.

ADRIAN: I try. I really do. But some skirt comes into the office.. Advertising is like that, you know. You get the top drawer totty. Models.

MEL: Models. Right. And you're the artist..

ADRIAN: (INTERRUPTING) Designer. I'm a fuckin designer. Artists are ten a fuckin penny. I'll tell you what artists do: stick a rabbit's foot in formaldehyde and call it Lucky.

MEL: But you're also a writer. In a way..?

ADRIAN: *Copy*writer. It's the only sort of writer people can trust these days. I sell things, mate. Keep the economy going. That's a moral imperative. Without people like me, well... I have to win the trust of the public. So. Where was I?

MEL: Models.

ADRIAN: Models. Presenters. Actresses. Models who act. Actresses who present. Presenters who model. And they look at me with those big cow eyes.

MEL: Right.

ADRIAN: And those... (GESTURES TO INDICATE LARGE BREASTS) ...udders.

MEL: Right. (TO AUDIENCE) Ade was well into farmyard metaphors by now. But clearly all was not well in the Big Avocado. I could see the anguish behind the bright lights. I could see that money and loveless sex had started to pall. What could I do? Then I had an idea. (TO ADRIAN) I've got an idea.

ADRIAN: (SURPRISED) You? (BEAT) What?

MEL: You should come back to Yorkshire where life's real. You could be happy again. There's plenty of advertising agencies in Leeds. (TO AUDIENCE) There *were* in those days! (BEAT) I never thought he'd agree to it.

ADRIAN: Tell me, young merkin, why would I do a fuckin stupid thing like that?

MEL: Because you could be happy.

ADRIAN: Happy? Like you?

MEL: Like me and Beatrice.

LIGHTS GO DOWN. MEL RETURNS TO FRONT OF STAGE. SPOTLIGHT.

MEL: (TO AUDIENCE) Well, I made my pitch – as they say in the circles in which I move. Or used to. (BEAT) I never really thought he'd do it.

BEATRICE MOVES INTO SPOTLIGHT

BEATRICE: You better sit down. I've got some news.

MEL: (EXCITED) You're not..? (HE FEELS HER STOMACH)

BEATRICE: (TURNING AWAY) At *my* age? Perish the thought.

MEL: Oh right. (BEAT) Then what.. ?

BEATRICE: I had a funny phone call.

MEL: You should get on to the phone company right away. Or the phone police. I'm sure I read in the Telegraph there are phone police these days especially for...

BEATRICE: (INTERRUPTING) Not that sort of call.

MEL: What sort of call then?

BEATRICE: A friend of yours. Said he was coming over to see you. To see *us*.

MEL: Well? What's wrong with that? That's good, isn't it?

BEATRICE: Ten o'clock on a Sunday morning isn't good. Sundays are my day of rest.

MEL: It does seem a funny time.

BEATRICE: I don't even look at a clean pair of knickers until well past one o'clock. Not on a Sunday.

MEL: What's his name?

BEATRICE: He's the one you met in London. The one you told me about. The artist. The one with the problems. The romantic problems. The drink problems.

MEL: No, no, he's a designer. And a copywriter. He doesn't like being called an artist.

BEATRICE: He'll like whatever he gets if he comes round here on a Sunday morning. I said we could only offer him coffee. He said that was all he wanted.

MEL: So what's he doing up here?

BEATRICE: He's starting a new life. Said it's all down to you. He's got a job in Leeds with Machin & Machin.

MEL: (ASTONISHED) He took my advice?

BEATRICE: That's the bit that scares me. (BEAT) There'll be some other reason we don't know about. Rape, murder, stealing a policeman's helmet...

MEL: Well, you'll still have to make him welcome.

BEATRICE: I suppose *we* will. (SHE LEAVES THE SPOTLIGHT AREA)

MEL: (TO AUDIENCE) Who'd've believed that he'd take my advice? (BEAT) But I could see Beatrice wasn't keen on meeting him, not keen at all. I guess it's the way some married women are – they tend to be very jealous of their husband's friends.

MEL EXITS STAGE RIGHT. SPOT GOES OUT, LIGHTS COME ON BACK OF STAGE REVEALING SETTEE AND CHAIR. BEATRICE IS SITTING ON SETTEE. THERE IS A COFFEE POT AND SET OF CUPS ON A TRAY ON THE TABLE. SOUND OF DOORBELL

MEL: (DISEMBODIED VOICE) I'll get it!

ENTER MEL AND ADRIAN STAGE RIGHT, ENTER BEATRICE STAGE LEFT

MEL: Beloved, this is Adrian, my best friend at school.

ADRIAN: (TAKING BEATRICE'S HAND) He said you were beautiful but he didn't do you justice. (HE SUDDENLY KISSES BEATRICE ON THE MOUTH AND THEY STAY FROZEN IN THE CLINCH)

MEL: (TO AUDIENCE) Adie always did that with women. None of this peck on the cheek business. (BEAT) I don't think Beatrice liked it much.

ADRIAN: (TO BEATRICE AS HE FINALLY BREAKS AWAY) One of many, I should add. One of the many friends that young Mel had in those days. Quite the centre of attention he was, this young man. None of us had any doubt that he'd get on in the world and marry a beautiful woman.

BEATRICE: (TAKING HER HAND AWAY) Really? We don't see many of them these days. Don't see many of your old schoolfriends, do we, Mel?

ADRIAN: And isn't that the sadness of life? Brothers in arms in life's quest for knowledge and wisdom, we all go our separate ways in the end. *Is nothing eternal?* I often ask myself. Love, friendship, passion? The value of the pound against a basket of currencies? (BEAT) Why does it all run away from us? What fault is it within our selves that allows this to happen?

BEATRICE: Maybe we talk too much.

ADRIAN: (AMUSED) Maybe we do.

BEATRICE: So why did you really come back north?

MEL: (TO AUDIENCE) Oh dear. Well, I had to give Beatrice one of my hard looks. (LOOKS HARD AT BEATRICE, LOOKS BACK AT AUDIENCE) I don't ask my wife to like everybody *I* like, but I *do* ask her to pretend a bit.

ADRIAN: (TO BEATRICE) I just got sick of life in the Metropolis. Truth is: those southerners don't know how to live. It's rush, rush, rush, get it done, get it done, do something else, go back to where you started, do it all again. Money, money, money. I've never been that way myelf.

BEATRICE: (SARCASTICALLY) What is this life if, full of care...

ADRIAN: ...we have no time to stand and stare? (TO MEL) She's not just a beauty, is she, Mel? She knows poetry. She has a way with language.

ADRIAN SITS ON THE SETTEE. BEATRICE SITS NEXT TO HIM. MEL SITS ON THE CHAIR. BEATRICE POURS THE COFFEE AND HANDS IT ROUND. THEY SIT IN SILENCE FOR A WHILE. ALL THE TIME ADRIAN WATCHES BEATRICE AND OCCASIONALLY THEIR EYES MEET AND SHE LOOKS AWAY, EMBARRASSED. MEL MERELY STARES OUT AT THE AUDIENCE AND TAPS HIS FINGERS ON THE ARM OF THE CHAIR. THEN ADRIAN LOOKS AT HIS WATCH, GETS TO HIS FEET

ADRIAN: Well, fortunate Mel and beautiful Beatrice, here is my fond adieu. Till the next time. The coffee was splendid and the company delightful. (HE SMILES, KISSES HER HAND AND EXITS STAGE RIGHT)

MEL: (CALLING AFTER HIM): It was only instant. The coffee. (TO BEATRICE) I know you like your Sunday mornings. I know you like it if we stay in bed with the Sunday Times. But you could have been a bit more...

BEATRICE: ...willing? (SHE LAUGHS) Oh come on. You don't think I drove him away, do you? You don't think that's why he left?

MEL: Well...

BEATRICE: You know why he came at this time, don't you? Because the pubs are shut. It's the only time he can be sure of being sober. Now it's a quarter to twelve and he's off to get pissed. He was never going to stay to lunch. Not even if we'd offered.

MEL: (TO AUDIENCE) I *do* think women are very hard sometimes. (BEAT) Anyway, it was summer. Or as close to summer as you ever get in Leeds, and it wasn't long before we met up with Adie again.

LIGHTS GO DOWN AT BACK OF STAGE AND UP AT THE FRONT AS MEL AND BEATRICE WALK INTO THEM

MEL: It was a Saturday night in August at a party given by the Denis Blakeneys. We always call Denis and Kate the Denis Blakeneys because we're friendly with another couple called Billy and Eloise Blakeney and we always call them the Billy Blakeneys.

BEATRICE: (GAZING OFF STAGE LEFT) Isn't that your friend Adrian? Who's he with?

MEL: (FOLLOWING HER GAZE THEN TURNING TO AUDIENCE) I was surprised to see Adie there. I'd been round to his little *pied-a-terre* a couple of times with a bottle of something and met him once at Dregs – you remember that's the wine bar that used to be the Japanese restaurant and was later kidnapped by Oxfam. I didn't know that Adie knew the Denis Blakeneys but it turned out he was seeing this girl – Crystal she was called – who was Kate Blakeney's cousin by marriage. She was at least 15 years younger than Adie and very pretty in my opinion and wore one of those party dresses that show a little bit, you know.. (GESTURES WITH HIS HANDS TO INDICATE BREASTS) and she was basically OK. I thought she was very nice.

ENTER ADRIAN AND CRYSTAL STAGE LEFT, ADRIAN STAGGERING SLIGHTLY, AND TRYING TO LIGHT A CIGARETTE, CRYSTAL SUPPORTING HIM

ADRIAN: (VERY LOUDLY) Mel! Beatrice! Beatrice! Mel! (THE CIGARETTE FALLS FROM HIS MOUTH AND HE PUTS HIS LIGHTER AWAY)

MEL: (TO AUDIENCE): He was a bit loud. (TO BEATRICE) Oh dear.

ADRIAN: (TO CRYSTAL IN A SLURRED VOICE) Here, girl, make yourself useful. (HE DISENTANGLES HIMSELF FROM HER AND HANDS HER HIS BRANDY GLASS) You, young sir, I'll shake your hand! (HE SHAKES MEL'S HAND)

MEL: (TO AUDIENCE): True to his word, he shook my hand..

ADRIAN GOES ON AND ON AND ON SHAKING MEL'S HAND

MEL: (EVENTUALLY TO AUDIENCE) He shook my hand in this exaggerated way, sort of pump-pumping away, not letting go. And then he seemed to get tired of that all of a sudden...

ADRIAN LEAVES MEL, WALKS OVER TO BEATRICE, TAKES HER HAND AS HE DID BEFORE AND AGAIN GIVES HER A KISS ON THE MOUTH, THIS TIME EVEN MORE LINGERING. MEL WATCHES THEM WITH HIS HAND STILL PUMPING AWAY AS THOUGH GUIDED BY AN OUTSIDE FORCE. FINALLY HE CATCHES HIMSELF DOING IT AND STOPS.

MEL: (TO AUDIENCE) I knew Beatrice didn't like it. But she made more of an effort this time.

BEATRICE: (EVENTUALLY BREAKING AWAY) Don't you think you'd better introduce us?

ADRIAN: Oh yes, yes. (HE GOES BACK TO CRYSTAL, RETRIEVES HIS GLASS THEN SAYS TO EVERYONE IN TURN) Crystal, Mel. Mel, Crystal. Beatrice, Crystal. Crystal,

Beatrice. (HE LINGERS OVER BEATRICE'S NAME AND LOOKS HER OVER)

MEL: (WAVING) Hello, Crystal.

CRYSTAL: (AWKWARD AND GUSHING AT THE SAME TIME) Hello. Hi. Really nice to meet you.

ADRIAN: Oh, seeing you two has really made my evening, you have no idea! You have rescued me from the terrors of the cybermen. I was caught up with a *clutch* of computer buffs. (TO BEATRICE) Is *clutch* the correct collective noun for computer buffs? I know you know your stuff when it comes to the English Language...

BEATRICE: It will do. *Clutch* will do.

ADRIAN: Yes, yes, it will do, lovely lady. (BEAT) Anyway, this clutch of morons have – sorry, has – no idea about life. That's *has* because *clutch* would be a singular noun. And they're all very singular people. Their notion of excitement – and I can say *their* because I am now talking about the computer crowd as individuals...

BEATRICE: It doesn't matter.

ADRIAN: (GAZING AT HER FONDLY) Doesn't matter?

BEATRICE: I don't seriously think you want to know this. But, just for the record, a collective noun can be used as either singular or plural. You can say a crowd of drunks *is* deeply depressing or a crowd of drunks *are* deeply depressing and both statements are correct.

ADRIAN: (SMILING TO MEL) Your wife is terrific. I hope you know how lucky you are.

MEL: Yes, well, I do. I...

ADRIAN: (INTERRUPTING) Anyway, this gaggle of gigaheads is, or are, as the case may be, comparing rival software systems in a soul-stirring quest to create the very model of a modern company account system. And that's the problem with company men – in reality, they're no company at all!

ADRIAN AND BEATRICE LAUGH AT HIS JOKE

ADRIAN: Well, Mrs Simmons, I never guessed you had such a beautiful laugh..

BEATRICE: You've never struck me as vaguely funny before.

MEL: (WALKING ACROSS TO CRYSTAL) What did *you* think? Were you bored as well?

CRYSTAL: (VERY SHY) Well, I try my best, you know. I do all I can to…

.

ADRIAN: Of course she wasn't bored. She loves parties. Don't you, Crystal? *Any* parties, *all* parties, the *stout* party, the Labour Party, the party of the first...

CRYSTAL TURNS AND STARTS TO WALK AWAY BUT HE REACHES ACROSS AND GRABS HER ARM

ADRIAN: Oh, for God's sake, Crystal, what's the matter?

CRYSTAL: (SHE STARTS TO CRY) He doesn't take any notice of me! (SHE PULLS AWAY AND RUNS OFFSTAGE LEFT)

ADRIAN: (SHOUTING) Don't walk away when I'm talking!

MEL: (STRIDES ACROSS TO HIM) Adrian, I have to say this. You can be very rude sometimes. Yes you can. (RAISES A FINGER TO PRE-EMPT DISAGREEMENT) You see, I may not know very much about art, or design, or collective nouns, but I do know a bit about computers. And I know enough about computers – and accounting – to know that we depend on these IT people nowadays. And that *you* are talking crap.

ADRIAN: But I carry it off, don't I? I always carry it off. Sometimes beautifully.

MEL: (HE DROPS HIS VOICE): Well, I just wonder how those computer chaps you've just been talking to in this very room maybe only five minutes ago, would take your snide references now. I mean, I don't hear any computer talk at the moment so I am unable to identify who it was to whom you were talking or if they are still within earshot. You always have to be careful who might be listening. You have to be aware of what's going on around you if you want..

BEATRICE: (SHOUTING OUT) Mel, help him!

AS SHE SPEAKS, ADRIAN COLLAPSES INTO MEL'S ARMS. MEL STRUGGLES TO HOLD ON TO HIM. BEATRICE RUSHES ACROSS TO HELP.

BEATRICE: Get him outside!

MEL: Yes. Fresh air. Do him some good. Bring him round.

BEATRICE: Find him some place to spew. I'll try to find the girlfriend and have a little word.

EXIT BEATRICE STAGE LEFT IN A HURRY. LIGHTS GO DOWN, THEN UP STAGE RIGHT, JUST ENOUGH FOR MOONLIGHT, REVEALING A BENCH. SOUNDS OF TRAFFIC. MEL HALF CARRIES ADRIAN TO THE BENCH AND THEY SIT DOWN. ADRIAN FLOPS OVER AND LIES WITH HIS HEAD IN MEL'S LAP. MEL IS CLEARLY EMBARRASSED.

MEL: Adie, Adie, why do you do it?

ADRIAN STIRS. HE RAISES HIS HEAD, HE SLUMPS BACKWARDS, HE RIGHTS HIMSELF. HE SEEMS TO BE COMING ROUND.

ADRIAN: Aaaaghhh!

MEL: You've got yourself a lovely girl there, you know that? I mean, from what I saw. Not that I know her very well. Not yet. But I could tell. A lovely girl.

ADRIAN: (BOOZILY) Lovely girl. Right. Too good for me. Compassionate. Cries a lot.

MEL: And I don't know why you want to go around offending people. Computer people aren't evil, you know.

ADRIAN: Aaah. Software. Cyberspace. Gigabytes. (PAUSE) Intellectual property rights.

MEL: (BRIGHTENING) Hey. Now you're talking. That's something I actually know a lot about...

ADRIAN: You have performed an illegal operation and your brain is about to shut down.

MEL: What?

ADRIAN FLOPS OVER ON HIS LEFT

MEL: How many have you had?

ADRIAN FLOPS OVER ON HIS RIGHT

MEL: How long do you really think you can carry on drinking like this?

ADRIAN: (SUDDENLY SITTING BOLT UPRIGHT AND STARING HARD AT MEL DEFIANTLY) Till my eyes bleed.

MEL: Oh dear. (TO AUDIENCE) I told you he was good with words. When Adie said something, it was always pretty memorable.

SUDDENLY ADRIAN TURNS AND VOMITS OVER THE BACK OF THE BENCH. MEL TURNS AWAY IN HORROR

MEL: Why do you do it, Adie? You're such a smart fella, you've got so much going for you.

ADRIAN SLUMPS UNCONSCIOUS ON THE BENCH AS BEATRICE RE-ENTERS STAGE LEFT

BEATRICE: I've called a taxi. There's a firm just round the corner.

MEL: Is Crystal taking him home?

BEATRICE: Is she fuck! I think Crystal is a little bit shattered right now. All she could say was (MIMICS CRYSTAL'S WHINE) I tried my best, I did all I could. (REVERTS TO REAL VOICE) I ask you! Silly bitch.

MEL: I'll go with him then. I'll go in the taxi.

BEATRICE: Will you fuck! Don't forget why you're here. You've got lots of potential clients who need to be warned about the effects of the European copyright laws on next year's business plans. You stick to what you have to do. I'll get him home. You write down the address. Nobody here is going to miss me.

MEL: *I'll* miss you.

BEATRICE: You can always have me later.

MEL SEARCHES IN HIS TROUSER POCKETS FOR PEN AND PAPER, WRITES DOWN ADRIAN'S ADDRESS. CAR HEADLIGHTS AND SOUNDS STAGE RIGHT INDICATE THE ARRIVAL OF THE TAXI. MEL AND BEATRICE CARRY ADRIAN OFFSTAGE RIGHT. THERE IS THE SOUND OF FOOTSTEPS, CAR DOORS AND THE TAXI ENGINE REVS UP. THE HEADLIGHTS DISAPPEAR. THE ONLY LIGHTS LEFT ARE FRONT STAGE. MEL RE-ENTERS STAGE RIGHT AND WALKS INTO THE LIGHT

MEL: (TO AUDIENCE) I wouldn't want you thinking my wife swears a lot. She doesn't. That was a very rare episode, believe me. But there are occasions in life when you have to be honest.

And tonight is one of them. (BEAT) Anyway, Adrian's the sort of chap that would make *anybody* swear. (BEAT) And it wasn't a bad night for me, not once he'd gone. Two of the people I buttonholed agreed I could phone them during the week and I was eager to tell Beatrice how well I'd done thanks to her. But, as it happened, I was back earlier than *she* was. So the wait was quite frustrating. When she did get back, I was pretty tired, I don't mind telling you.

HE TAKES OFF HIS SHOES AND STARTS TO TAKE OFF HIS SHIRT. ENTER BEATRICE STAGE RIGHT

BEATRICE: God, I'm tired. That man is a big baby. (SHE TAKES OFF HER SHOES) Also a big heavy lump when he's out cold like that. I don't know how you two ever got to be friends.

MEL: You were a long time. Give you any trouble, did he? He didn't spew again?

BEATRICE: If he *had* done, I'd've taken his head off with a breadknife.

MEL: Oh, don't be so hard on him. You've not seen him at his best. (PAUSE, HE SMOOCHES UP TO HER) I'd be upset if you and Adie didn't get along.

BEATRICE: He's a waster. That's what's so terrible – the waste. Not worth bothering about. Not worth getting caught up in. And that stupid girl – *I did all I could, but he doesn't take any notice of me* (BEAT) Sorry, Mel. I'm really tired. We'll do it in the morning. I promise. (SHE WALKS OFF INTO DARKNESS)

MEL: (TO AUDIENCE) So I didn't get to tell her how well I'd done. Not right then, anyway. Saved it all till later. (PAUSE WHILE HE BUTTONS UP HIS SHIRT AND PUTS HIS SHOES BACK ON) After that, we didn't see much of Adie for a while. Well, you can understand why Bea wouldn't go near him again after all the trouble, and I didn't feel it was right for me to push her. But I actually heard from mutual friends (GESTURES INTO AUDIENCE) – I think it was you actually, Charlie – that he was doing OK. Machin & Machin, as you probably know, was a very respected company that produced give-away newspapers for pubs. And Adie was running the whole operation. I suppose it was a subject close to his heart. And a little bit later there was a new girlfriend too. (BEAT) So I decided it was time to clear the air.

BEATRICE ENTERS STAGE LEFT

MEL: (TO BEATRICE): We could have them over one Sunday for dinner. (PAUSE) Look, give him another chance, will you? This new girl – Amy – everybody says she's really great and she's been so good for him. He's a changed man, believe me.

BEATRICE: I doubt that.

MEL: You don't know. You haven't seen him since the Denis Blakeneys' party. Haven't even spoken to him. Neither have I. I tell you he's a new man. (TO AUDIENCE): Well, I wore her down. I think really that she was quite interested to see the new love in Adrian's life. We finally agreed to ask them over for lunch the next available Sunday. This Amy was, by all accounts, pretty intelligent and taught primary school in Wakefield. (TO BEATRICE) And I believe she's quite a bit younger than Adrian.

BEATRICE: Well, there's a surprise.

MEL: You could talk to her about poetry.

BEATRICE: Why should I talk to her about poetry?

MEL: Teachers always like to talk about poetry.

BEATRICE: And what the fuck do I know about poetry?

MEL: Oh come on, everybody knows you know lots...

LIGHTS GO UP FURTHER BACK TO REVEAL SETTEE, CHAIR AND TABLE. THERE ARE FOUR WINE GLASSES ON THE TABLE. SOUND OF DOORBELL

MEL: (JUMPING TO IT) Right. I'll get it.

BEATRICE SITS ON SETTEE. MEL RE-ENTERS STAGE RIGHT WITH ADRIAN AND AMY. ADRIAN IS CARRYING AN ASDA BAG.

MEL: (TO ADRIAN AND AMY) Come in, come in! Beatrice, this is Amy.

ADRIAN: Amy, this is Beatrice.

MEL TAKES AMY'S COAT AND EXITS STAGE LEFT WITH IT. AMY SITS ON THE SETTEE WITH BEATRICE. MEL RETURNS AND SITS ON THE CHAIR. ADRIAN SITS ON THE FLOOR AND

GAZES SOLIDLY AT BEATRICE. THE OTHER THREE GLANCE BACK AND FORTH, SMILING AWKWARDLY IN THE SILENCE. THEN …

MEL: (TO AUDIENCE) We had a great time. Beatrice had done roast beef and Yorkshire with all the trimmings followed by apple pie and custard. She was clearly making an effort to please me. (BEAT) And this Amy was a real... well, pretty girl. Reminded me of someone. (BEAT) Anyway, it looked as if she had Adie under control. They'd brought a bottle of Rioja (ADRIAN TAKES THE BOTTLE OUT OF THE ASDA BAG AND HOLDS IT UP FOR THE AUDIENCE TO SEE) and some After-8 mints (ADRIAN ALSO SHOWS THESE TO THE AUDIENCE) even though it was the middle of the day

BEATRICE UNCORKS THE BOTTLE AND POURS THE WINE INTO THREE OF THE GLASSES

MEL: So after dinner we had a drink and a mint and Adrian drank …tonic water!

POINTS AND LAUGHS AS BEATRICE PRODUCES TUMBLER AND BOTTLE OF TONIC FROM BEHIND TABLE, POURS IT AND ADRIAN DRINKS IT

MEL: I couldn't believe it! I thought: thank you, Amy! And then we got to talking about... oh, just lots of things.

IN THE FOLLOWING EXCHANGES, MEL AND AMY STARE STRAIGHT OUT AT THE AUDIENCE. ADRIAN KEEPS HIS EYES ON BEATRICE, WHO LOOKS DOWN AT HER FEET.

ADRIAN: (GLANCING AT BEATRICE) Literature. (BEAT) Shall I compare thee to a summer's day?

AMY: Politics. (BEAT) I voted for Tony Blair the first time. But I'll not vote for Gordon Brown. Not after Northern Rock.

MEL: Business. (BEAT) It's often overlooked that some of the lesser known articles of the proposed European constitution will be in many ways beneficial to smaller firms in the UK. In fact, I think we're about to see a boom time for smaller businesses.

ADRIAN: Music. (BEAT) Ahh. The food of love.

AMY: Football. (BEAT) I think the press was very unfair to Steve McLaren. It's no wonder he quit. And now we've got this Italian. I'm not sure I'm keen on having a foreigner. It didn't work out with Sven.

MEL: Retail. (BEAT) The resurgence of Marks and Spencer as a major high street player was a major surprise to many people. Still, I always refused to sell my shares.

AMY: Well, it's a British institution.

ADRIAN: Painting. (BEAT) Why did Picasso want to turn women into triangles? Was it an obsession with pubic hair?

AMY: Africa. (BEAT) I blame American foreign policy for all of it.

MEL: Finance. (BEAT) Most of the bankers I know really earn their bonuses. And I'm sure the price of property will rise again. Well, you might see another small downturn before that happens, of course.

SILENCE. AFTER A MINUTE OR SO …

MEL: And then there was a lull. And I nudged Beatrice and I said – in a very quiet voice, of course, but I don't mind if *you* hear it. (TO BEATRICE) I was right, wasn't I? This one is going to be good for him. (TO AUDIENCE) And then somebody got onto the subject of...

BEATRICE: (FIRMLY TO AUDIENCE) Education.

AMY: (TO AUDIENCE) Education? Well, let me tell you what it's like. Government interference. All that bloody paperwork. Ticking boxes. Filling in endless reports. Never daring to suggest that any of the pupils – sorry, the students – might be anything less than perfect. I used to believe in our education system, but now I wonder..

MEL: (TO AUDIENCE) Now, I'm the sort of bloke who hates bureaucracy and it always seemed to me that Beatrice shared my opinions about Government interference. But she suddenly weighs in with some line about how a whole generation of teachers had failed their pupils. (PAUSE) Or should that be *its* pupils?

BEATRICE: (SUDDENLY VENOMOUS AND LEANING IN AMY'S FACE): It's the teachers' fault. Because discipline's disappeared. Classes are disrupted. And examinations have become utterly corrupt. Course work, indeed! Do it once, do it twice and before we send it in, we'll get the teacher to fill in the answers. Nobody trusts teachers, nobody respects them. How can anybody work in a place where there's no discipline or trust?

MEL: Hey, Beatrice, (LAUGHS, EMBARRASSED) I think that's pretty serious talk for Sunday afternoon.

BEATRICE: And it affects us all, doesn't it? It affects all of society. I mean, even if we don't have children..

MEL: Which we don't, of course. Not yet.

BEATRICE: If the teachers can't get a handle on it, the rest of us get the fallout. The crime, the unemployment! We're raising a generation of people who don't seem to know anything, who can't see what's really going on in society.

MEL: Which you could never say about *our* generation.

BEATRICE: What do young people know about money or making a living? If it's not on Facebook, it doesn't exist. That's why we're all in trouble now – because people can't tell the difference between reality and reality TV. They're actually buying debt. Like it was something you see in an Argos catalogue. All you need to do to make a killing these days is parcel up a bunch of IOUs and flog them to the highest bidder. You take a load of shit, put it in fancy packaging, and call it an opportunity. But one thing you can't do – you can't hide the stink.

AMY: (ANGRY NOW) But you can't blame teachers for the failures of society. (BEAT) It's the financial system that's at fault. Here we are, shovelling money into the banks to keep them afloat and the bankers are still creaming off their bloody bonuses. It's...

BEATRICE: (INTERRUPTING) What do *you* think, Adrian?

ADRIAN: (QUIETLY, DEADLY SERIOUS FOR ONCE) What do I think? Well (PAUSE) I think if you have capitalism, you'll always have recession. It's like with religion. If you have religion, you've got to have hell. You can't have one without the other. (CATCHING HIMSELF, SUDDENLY ATTEMPTING TO CHANGE THE SUBJECT AND LIGHTEN THE MOOD) Hey, Mel, young business brain of the year, at least one of us is still doing well. (HE PUTS DOWN HIS SLIMLINE TONIC) I hear you've got lots of new contracts out of this European legislation stuff. Half a dozen was what I heard. So somebody's still living off the fat of the land, thank God.

MEL: Well, yes I have. I'm glad you mentioned that, Adie. (BEAT) On the night of the Denis Blakeneys' party, I got a strong hint from you that you found my line of work fairly uninteresting. (BEAT) How did you know I'd got lots of new contracts?

LONG PAUSE, THEN ...

ADRIAN: I don't know. Someone must have told me.

MEL: Well, not many people knew...

BEATRICE: (SUDDENLY SUBDUED) *I* might have told a couple of people...

ADRIAN: (HESITANTLY) And those people must have told *me*. (BEAT) These things get around. Success stories always do in times of uncertainty. Spread like wildfire.

MEL: (SMILES) Well, that's my wife for you. She's always supportive, always proud of the things I do. Marriage is a great thing, you know.

ADRIAN: Yes.

MEL: Trust. Stability. Something to build your life on. I'd recommend it to anybody.

AMY: (LOOKING ACROSS TO MEL) You really don't know, do you? (MORE LOUDLY)You really don't know...

ADRIAN: (INTERRUPTING) ...just how much we follow your career!

LIGHTS DIM AND SPOTS COME UP AT FRONT OF STAGE. MEL AND BEATRICE MOVE INTO THE SPOTLIGHT

MEL: (TO THE AUDIENCE) I was pleased with the way things had gone. (TO BEATRICE) I think that went really well. (PAUSE, EYES STONEY-FACED BEATRICE) Well, I think it went *allright*. Certainly nothing less than allright. And did you see Adie's driving them home? I don't think I've ever seen him drive anybody home from a party before.

BEATRICE: Hardly a party.

MEL: Well, you were a bit aggressive during the Great Education Debate. Maybe next time you'll go a little easier on the girl.

BEATRICE: I don't think there'll *be* a next time. I don't think she's the one for him. (SHE EXITS STAGE RIGHT)

MEL: (TO AUDIENCE) And you know what? Beatrice was right. I bumped into Crystal Blakeney at Dregs. You remember Dregs? (BEAT) Yes, of course you do. Anyway, Crystal was going out with some chap from my office. And they told me about Adie and Amy, how their big relationship had suddenly gone down the pan. She said Adie was in the bar on his own one night going through a re-run of his routine about women being too good for him and something about how he didn't deserve to have any *friends* either. (BEAT) And ten days later he was (BEAT) dead.

WOMAN'S SOBBING HEARD IN BACKGROUND, MEL LOOKS ROUND EMBARRASSED

MEL: The inquest said open verdict because they couldn't be sure whether Adie jumped from the top floor of the car park or just fell off, considering all the booze inside him. But why should he kill himself? OK, his big romance had broken up. But he'd been through that sort of thing before and he'd always got over it. On the other hand, Machin & Machin had gone into liquidation because of all the pubs that were closing down. (BEAT) The coroner said it was a blessing Adie hadn't been able to get to his car, which meant other lives may well have been saved. I thought that was pretty unfeeling. (BEAT) I remembered then that thing Adie said to me once: The ground broke my fall. He was always good at little phrases that stuck in the mind.

BEATRICE RE-ENTERS STAGE RIGHT, RED-FACED, HOLDING BACK THE TEARS, DABBING HER EYES WITH A HANDKERCHIEF

MEL: Even Beatrice was put out by Adie's death. I thought it was a shame she'd never got to know him better. (BEAT) So. A talented chap like Adie who had everything – brains, looks, charm – he just couldn't cut it. But an ordinary bloke like me, who marries a good wife, ends up happy and fulfilled. (BEAT) I tried to say this to Beatrice, to sort of thank her for everything. I said: (HE TURNS TO FACE HER) I want you to know I'll always be here for you. And I hope you'll always be here for me. (TO AUDIENCE) And it was lovely. She just smiled and said…

BEATRICE: (STONY-FACED, TO AUDIENCE) Till my eyes bleed.

SILENCE, THEN …

MEL: (TO AUDIENCE) Well. Thanks to all of you for coming. Thank you! (WAVES, THEN SHOUTS) Terry boy, how d'you think it went?

TERRY: (FROM THE AUDIENCE) As well as could be expected, Mel.

MEL: Thanks, mate. (BEAT) Now I can see my good lady is a bit tired and emotional so it really is time to finish. (TO AUDIENCE) Oh Blanche, you'll have to tell Beatrice which diet you've been on, because you look so good. I bet you can't wait to get scoffing things again, right? (BEAT) And Terry, I know you didn't really get banned. Thought I'd better make that plain in case there's somebody here tonight might take it seriously. (BEAT) So. Nothing left to say except thanks for coming. Thanks for coming, all of you. (BEAT) OK, let's remember we're here to be happy! A bit more music then. Come on!

LIGHTS DIM, SPOTLIGHT ON. REHAB BY AMY WINEHOUSE IS PLAYED. MEL GRABS BEATRICE AND DANCES WITH HER ALTHOUGH SHE CONSTANTLY TRIES TO PULL AWAY FROM HIM. THEY DANCE FRANTICALLY ROUND AND ROUND THE STAGE. SUDDENLY MUSIC STOPS AND THEY FREEZE, BEATRICE STONY-FACED, MEL SMILING IDIOTICALLY.

SPOTLIGHT OFF.

END

Sunday Afternoon Again

...was selected for the Write Now Liverpool One-Act Drama Festival and performed there by the Sandal Theatre Company in April 2012. Cast and crew:

Lenny.. Brox Baslow
Dad.. Robert Boyle
Mam.. Rachel Ashton
Nan... Pat Brocklehurst

Directed by Martha Simon
Assistant Director Kathryn Docherty
Running time: 60 minutes

Characters

Lenny, an educated middle class man in his sixties who also plays himself as a boy of eight but does not change his physical appearance or dress – only his behaviour, switching between exaggerated childishness and detached old age.

Mam, mother of Lenny, middle thirties, lower middle class, dowdy, speaks standard English

Dad, father of Lenny, middle thirties, working class, fat, speaks broad Yorkshire

Nan, mother of Lenny's mother, old, aggressive, lower middle class, small but sturdy, speaks standard English

Plus the following characters are pre-recorded voice only: **A group** of working class children singing; **Jean Metcalfe**, radio presenter; **The Lone Ranger**, masked avenger of the west; **Tonto**, his faithful Indian companion; **Billy Cotton**, cockney radio band show host.

Pre-recorded music and effects including: the Andre Kostelanetz orchestra, the Billy Cotton band, the cry of Tarzan, traffic sounds, radio static, an air raid siren, Ella Fitzgerald singing *Every Time We Say Goodbye,* Fred Astaire singing *Top Hat.*

Setting: A council house Sheffield, Yorkshire. The stage is divided into two halves: living room (stage right) and kitchen (stage left).

Time: Coronation Year 1953.

Furniture: Two armchairs. A small table and a wooden chair. (NB To keep furniture to a minimum, the living room chairs can be simple wooden chairs covered by throws to suggest "armchairness". I have included a stage direction for characters to remove the throws, turning the armchairs into wooden chairs, and carry them across from living room to kitchen.)

Props: Pillow, walking stick, frying pan, kettle, teapot, two cups, tea tray, pair of men's shoes, cardboard box containing shoe polish, cloth and brush, Brycreem jar and hair brush, shoe box containing sepia postcard-size photos held by rubber bands, three dinner plates, three sets of knive and forks, one pudding bowl, one dessert spoon, brown paper carrier bag, pop bottle, tumbler, towel, packet of aniseed balls, bottle Lea & Perrin's Worcester sauce, Lenny's pile of comics including The Lone Ranger and Tarzan, The Daily Mirror newspaper 1953, any time after June, The People newspaper, 1953, any time after June.

STAGE IN DARKNESS. THEN PIERCING SCREAM OF A CHILD. PAUSE. THEN ENTER LENNY STAGE RIGHT IN SPOTLIGHT, DRESSED IN MODERN CASUAL ADULT CLOTHES. HE IS SUCKING HIS THUMB AND CARRYING A PILLOW UP AGAINST HIS FACE. HE GOES TO CENTRE FRONT OF STAGE, TAKES THUMB OUT OF MOUTH

LENNY: (TO AUDIENCE) Sorry about that. Should've warned you. That's me. Screaming. That's me. Lenny. (BEAT) I know it doesn't *sound* like me, not the way I sound now. That's because I was only eight years old in those days. Coronation year!

MAM'S VOICE: (SHOUTING) Lenny! Lenny! What's the matter, my love?

LENNY: That's me mam. (SMILES, LISTENS ATTENTIVELY)

DAD'S VOICE : (SHOUTING) Ey up, son! Don't tek on so!

LENNY: That's me dad. (SMILES, LISTENS ATTENTIVELY)

NAN'S VOICE: (FORCEFUL BUT NOT REALLY SHOUTING) Leonard! What's all this row? Don't you know what time it is, young man? It's middle of the night. You'll wake the dead with all your nonsense.

LENNY: (GRINS) That's me nan. (BEAT) My mother's mother. Grandma Guthrie. Me dad's mam was long dead by this time. Nobody lives long in *his* family. Except me.

SOUND OF TAPPING – THREE TAPS, WOOD ON WOOD

LENNY: And that's me nan's walking stick.

THREE TAPS REPEATED

LENNY: There it is again. (BEAT) You'll get used to it.

ENTER MAM AND DAD STAGE LEFT IN SPOT, BOTH WEARING DRESSING GOWNS. THEY LOOK WORRIED

MAM: He's had a bad dream. But he'll be allright. Won't you, Lenny?

ENTER NAN, ALSO STAGE LEFT IN SPOT, CARRYING WALKING STICK, SHE IS ALSO WEARING DRESSING GOWN

MAM: (PLACATING NAN) He'll be allright, mother.

DAD: (DISMISSIVE) Lad's had a bit of a dream, that's all.

LENNY: (STARTS TO CRY, HOLDS PILLOW TO HIS FACE, CONTINUES SUCKING THUMB) She was here! The witch! The witch was here! In my room! Sitting on the chair! Looking at me!

LIGHTS GO UP ALL OVER STAGE, REVEALING STAGE RIGHT TWO CHAIRS COVERED BY THROWS, STAGE LEFT SMALL KITCHEN TABLE COVERED BY CLOTH PLUS CHAIR.

MAM: There, there. It's a dream.

DAD: What's the lad on about? What's he on about now?

MAM: It's the woman down the road. It's a kids' thing. It's nothing.

DAD: It *looks* like bloody nothing.

LENNY: (STILL DISTRAUGHT) She was here! She got in the house! She got in my room!

MAM: It's a dream, that's all it is.

NAN: Well, I'm getting back to my bed.

MAM TAKES OFF HER DRESSING GOWN, REVEALING CARDIGAN AND SKIRT. DAD TAKES OFF HIS DRESSING GOWN REVEALING SWEATER AND TROUSERS. NAN TAKES THE DRESSING GOWNS AND PILLOW AND EXITS STAGE LEFT

LENNY: (TO AUDIENCE) Dream? It was no dream! (BEAT) I was only eight years old, but I knew a few things. (BEAT) Witches, for instance. I knew a witch when I saw one. There was one down our street. All the kids knew she was a witch.

CHILD VOICES: (SING-SONG) Mrs Croome, Mrs Croome, fly to Barnsley on your silly old broom!

LENNY: (TO AUDIENCE) She was tall and thin, with long arthritic fingers. Though I didn't know the word *arthritic*, not in those days. I do *now*. (STRETCHES OUT HIS HAND, LOOKS AT IT) Believe me, I really do now. (BEAT) And she always wore black, so you knew what she was, you couldn't miss it. A long black frock and a black shawl draped across her head like a nun's cowl. (BEAT) But when I told my mam and dad, they just laughed.

DAD: It's only Mrs Croome down the road. She's eighty-nine. She's no more a witch than your mam is. Or your nan. She's no more a witch than *I* am. There's no such things as witches.

MAM: Lenny, you should mind your manners when you talk about Mrs Croome. (TO DAD) It's a silly kids' thing, that's all.

CHILD VOICES: (OVERLAPPING, SHOUTING ACROSS EACH OTHER) Acky one two three! Bags not on! You're on! I'm not! I tigged you! You're on, you are! Stupid kid! Stupid Lenny!

LENNY: (SHOUTING) No, I'm not! No, I'm not! I'm *not* stupid! And I'm not *on*! I'm *not* on! I'm *not* on! So *there*! (TO AUDIENCE) I was *always* on when we played tig. You see, I could never run fast. Even if I tigged somebody, they always tigged me back before I could run away. I hated it. (BEAT) Anyway, I had other things to think about. I had to keep a look out. For *her*. For Mrs Croome. (BEAT) When I played with my pals, Tommy and Denis, or when I went with mam to Tordoff's, the shop on the corner, I kept watching out for the witch. As soon as I saw that black hooded figure in the distance, I'd go scurrying away into our back yard and bang on the door for me mam to let me in. (BEAT) I didn't know exactly what it was that witches did to little boys, but I knew how she must hate me for knowing what she was.

MAM: Witches, Lenny! Honestly! (BEAT) Just listen to the boy! Where does he get it from?

DAD: Well, don't look at *me*! He don't get it off *me*! (TO LENNY) Tha wants to watch it, lad. Else tha's gonna grow up daft if tha believes daft things!

LENNY: (TO AUDIENCE) What did *they* know? What did any of the grown-ups know? (BEAT) Oh, they were clever enough at some things. When it came to digging the garden…

DAD: We'll have cabbages next to them turnips!

LENNY: … putting up fences, laying out the lawn, oh, they knew their stuff then! But they didn't know what *danger* was! *Their* idea of danger was to go on all the time about the traffic…

MAM: Don't go playing football at the end of Francis Street. The way those cars come flying out of there…!

LENNY: (TO AUDIENCE) They were *silly*! That was the only way I could put it. They knew nothing about the horrible spells the old witch was chanting every night. Only *I* could imagine that. (BEAT) It was all because of the war, this silliness.

SOUND OF AIR RAID SIREN

LENNY: I couldn't remember the war because I only just managed to be born in the last year of it. But it infected *all* the grown-ups. Sometimes, if I did something bad, and me dad took me aside to chastise me, he always started by telling me what a lucky boy I was.

DAD: (WAVING A FINGER) Tha's a lucky lad, Lenny. Tha doesn't know how lucky! Tha doesn't know tha's been born.

MAM: He doesn't. It's true. That's the honest truth.

DAD: He doesn't know how lucky the lot of us are…

MAM: No, he doesn't.

DAD: …living the way we do. (BEAT) Tha doesn't know what war is, our Lenny, tha just sees it on the films and it's bang bang and Erroll bloody Flynn and it's not like that at all. (RUBS AND FLEXES HIS ARM) Tha knows I nearly lost this arm in a burning tank in North Africa. It was the eve of Alamein. That's how I come to miss the battle. I'm only here today because some good muckers pulled me out. It took me months to get back the use of me muscles.

MAM: And you've not got all of it back. You've not got all the feeling. Those two fingers, you still can't use them properly….

DAD: (LAUGHS, DOES A V SIGN) Well, I only notice when I say goodnight to the foreman…

MAM: (SHARPLY) Don't be vulgar. I won't *have* it. Not in front of the boy!

DAD: But I'm trying to tell 'im. It's thanks to the National Ealth that I can use this arm at *all*. We never had that when I was a boy!

LENNY: (TO AUDIENCE) And then he'd go on about the years *before* the war…

DAD: I was one of the few that had jobs, young Lenny, being skilled, an electro-plater, when they had no doors on the lavatories at work and tha just had three minutes in and out or they docked thee pay.

LENNY: (TO AUDIENCE) That was me dad's history lesson. Only nowadays things were so much better.

DAD: That Edmund Hillary, climbing biggest mountain int' world, aren't you proud he's British?

MAM: And isn't the Queen beautiful? And she's so *young*. And didn't she do well at the Coronation?

LENNY: (TO AUDIENCE) And then they'd come to the point.

DAD: Tha mustn't kick that Sheila Whitehouse. Not even when she *starts* it. Because she's only a girl and boys don't hit girls.

LENNY: (SUDDENLY DEFIANT) *I* do.

DAD: (RAISING HIS HAND) Then tha'll get a smack from me! I'll make thee rue the day I ever got some feeling back in me arm. *Thee* will be the one to feel it then!

LENNY: (TO AUDIENCE) Everything was being built or re-built, like the half-finished street where we lived in our council house.

DAD: I still can't get over having a privy in the house…

MAM: It's not a privy, it's a bathroom. (BEAT) Grown men have died for it.

NAN ENTERS STAGE LEFT WITH STICK, WEARING CARDIGAN AND SKIRT. SHE HOBBLES ACROSS TO THE CHAIRS STAGE RIGHT AND SITS DOWN

LENNY: (TO AUDIENCE) Nothing here but fields two years ago. (BEAT) Everybody had just been born or *re*-born, and it was all because of the war. (BEAT) It seemed to me I was older than the grown-ups. And that's why I couldn't make them understand about witches.

MAM: It's Sunday again. Day of rest. Though not for some. Not for *me*. (TO DAD) I suppose *you'll* be going down the pub.

DAD: It's what I *do* of a Sunday.

LENNY: (TO AUDIENCE) I was only eight years old, but I knew what a pub was. I knew a pub even though I'd never been in one. There was a time, before nan had come to live with us, when mam and dad would go down the pub and I'd go as well.

SOUNDS OF TRAFFIC

DAD: (TO LENNY) Now lad, sit ’ere on t' side of step out of people's way an' I'll bring thee out some lemonade and crisps. Or would thee rather 'ave cheese biscuits?

LENNY: (TO AUDIENCE) I always asked for crisps. Then I'd drink the lemonade as slowly as I could, and eat the crisps one at a time, so I could stretch them out to fill the hours. Though sometimes it would be OK because I’d have *other* kids to talk to. Then we'd stand tiptoe up against the window and try to see in. (HE ACTS THIS OUT) You couldn't see much because the special glass was dirty white, like day-old snow, but where it said the name of the pub *The – Red – Dragon* (TRACES IT WITH HIS FINGER) it was clear, so you had to get really close and screw up your eyes and look through the strokes of the letters. You'd try to see mam and dad in the crowd of people, but you never could. Then you'd get tired from standing on your toes. (STANDS AT EASE, FACING THE AUDIENCE AGAIN)

MAM: (TO DAD) So you see, it’s the only thing to do. I’m the only one my mother’s got left. So she’ll *have* to come and live with us.

DAD: Well, I don’t know. It’s not as if we’ve got that much room. And will she get on with our Lenny?

MAM: Course she will. They’re very alike, Lenny and his nan. They even *look* alike.

DAD: *I’ve* never noticed it. (RESIGNED) Well, you’ve made up your mind to it then.

HE WALKS ACROSS TO STAGE LEFT, AND SITS ON CHAIR NEXT TO TABLE

MAM: (LOOKS HARD AT LENNY) Just a little something round the eyes. And the way they hold themselves…

LENNY: (TO AUDIENCE) It was a relief when nan *did* come to live because then there was always somebody to stay in the house with me. You'll have noticed she limps a bit. It was from the wound she'd got during the air raids on Sheffield. Which is why she'd got a walking stick.

LENNY RUNS ACROSS TO THE LIVING ROOM AND SITS IN FRONT OF NAN, LOOKS EXCITEDLY AT HER BUT SLIGHTLY TURNED SO THAT HE ALSO FACES THE AUDIENCE. IT IS OBVIOUS THAT HE LOVES HIS NAN.

LENNY: Show us your leg, nan, show us the hole.

NAN LAUGHS, PULLS UP HER SKIRT AND PULLS DOWN HER STOCKING

LENNY: (TO AUDIENCE) And there it was! The hole where the shrapnel went in! You can't see it where you are so I'll describe it! A full half-inch deep, two inches across, criss-crossed by little blue scars like veins in gorgonzola. (HE POINTS AT THE LEG AND LAUGHS)

MAM: You shouldn't *encourage* him, showing him things like that.

NAN: He's our Leonard. He has to know what we've been through. What we *still* go through.

LENNY GETS UP, STILL EXCITED, RUNS TO FRONT OF STAGE

LENNY: (TO AUDIENCE) But the outings to the pub got fewer. Even when dad *did* go out these days, mam most often stayed in. To keep nan company, she said. (BEAT) So that was a pub. That was where dad went Sunday mornings. (BEAT) Always the same. He'd get up early, and walk down to Tordoff's for the *Sunday Despatch* and *The People*, take me with him while mam and nan fried the breakfast. He always bought me some Rolo or aniseed balls. (HE TAKES THE SWEETS OUT OF HIS POCKET, UNWRAPS THEM AND STARTS EATING) Even though mam told him not to, that he'd spoil my appetite. (BEAT) When we got back, we'd have egg and bacon with tinned tomatoes and dad would do the washing up.

DAD STAGE LEFT PICKS UP FRYING PAN AND WALKS TO CENTRE STAGE

DAD: (TO LENNY) It's me Sunday job.

NAN AND MAM GET UP AND WALK TOWARDS DAD. HE HANDS MAM THE PAN. MAM AND NAN GO STAGE LEFT. NAN SITS DOWN AT TABLE, MAM PUTS FRYING PAN ON TOP OF TABLE, PICKS UP KETTLE, MIMES TURNING ON TAP, POURING WATER AND MAKING TEA WITH TEAPOT AND CUPS. NAN SITS AT TABLE, GAZES AHEAD OF HER, TAPS WALKING STICK THREE TIMES ON FLOOR. DAD WALKS STAGE RIGHT AND SITS IN NAN'S ARMCHAIR. HE PICKS UP A NEWSPAPER AND BEGINS TO READ

LENNY: (TO AUDIENCE) He'd *pretend* to read the paper. But you could tell he was waiting, waiting for it to be time.

THE FOLLOWING RITUAL OF DAD GROOMING HIMSELF FOR HIS EXCURSION TO THE PUB SHOULD BE SLOW WITH A FEEELING OF THE CEREMONIAL, ALMOST A KNIGHT PREOPARING FOR HIS QUEST

DAD: (CALLING OUT) Lenny, go and get my Sunday shoes, there's a good lad.

LENNY RUNS TO STAGE LEFT, RETURNS WITH SHOES, PLACES THEM IN FRONT OF DAD, SITS ON FLOOR IN FRONT OF HIM, LOOKING EXCITEDLY AT HIM, BUT AGAIN SLIGHTLY TURNED SO HE ALSO FACES THE AUDIENCE. IT IS OBVIOUS HE LOVES HIS DAD.

DAD: Lenny, go and get the blacking and the cloth.

LENNY GETS UP, RUNS TO STAGE LEFT, RETURNS WITH A CARDBOARD BOX FILLED WITH SHOE POLISH, CLOTH AND BRUSH, PLACES THEM ON FLOOR IN FRONT OF DAD, SITS ON FLOOR. DAD BEGINS TO TEAR UP THE NEWSPAPER

LENNY: (TO AUDIENCE) Don't worry! He's only tearing out the sports pages – the ones mam and nan never wanted to read.

DAD LAYS THE PAGES ON THE FLOOR IN FRONT OF HIM, PICKS UP SHOES, POLISH AND BRUSH, AND PERFORMS THE TASK OF CLEANING HIS SHOES IN A PERFUNCTORY WAY WHILE

LENNY'S COMMENTARY PROVIDES LOTS OF EXTRA DETAIL

LENNY: (TO AUDIENCE) After that, he'd lay everything out on the paper, take out the laces, turn the key on the Cherry Blossom. (BEAT) Always the same routine, dipping the brush in the polish, moving it across, smearing big black gobs on the bristles. He brushed each shoe in turn, short sharp jabs and circles. Then he took the rag, and –wait for it!

DAD SPITS ON SHOES THEN WIPES IT OFF WITH RAG

DAD: I know I shouldn't do it. Just don't tell thee mother I'm showin' thee dirty 'abits…

LENNY: (TO AUDIENCE) And he rubbed them till they shone like new! (HE CLAPS HIS HANDS IN WONDER)

DAD PUTS THE TOP BACK ON THE POLISH

DAD: Tek it back for us, our Lenny.

LENNY GETS UP, TAKES THE POLISH, CLOTH AND BRUSH, PUTS THEM BACK IN THE BOX, PICKS UP BOX AND AND RUNS BACK TO STAGE LEFT, DROPPING THEM OFF. DAD RUCKS UP THE PAPER ON THE FLOOR, THROWS IT OFFSTAGE, RETURNS TO CHAIR. LENNY RETURNS AND SITS IN FRONT OF HIS DAD AGAIN. MAM WALKS SLOWLY ACROSS FROM STAGE LEFT AND STANDS BEHIND LENNY, LOOKING AT DAD

MAM: (TO DAD) I've just come in to see you've not got polish on the suite. It's not as if we can afford a new one.

DAD: Polish ont' suite? You should know me better. (BEAT) I'll go and perform me ablutions.

HE WALKS TO STAGE LEFT, PAST NAN WHO FOLLOWS HIM WITH HER EYES AND TAPS HER WALKING STICK THREE TIMES AGAIN AS HE EXITS STAGE LEFT. WE HEAR DAD'S FOOTSTEPS ON THE STAIRS. LENNY GETS UP AND RUNS TO FRONT OF STAGE

LENNY: (TO AUDIENCE) After the shoes, he'd go upstairs to wash and shave. And the rest of us waited.

MAM STAGE RIGHT AND NAN STAGE LEFT FREEZE. LENNY WHISTLES TUNELESSLY AND TAPS HIS FOOT. THEN DAD'S FOOTSTEPS ON STAIRS AGAIN. DAD RE-ENTERS STAGE LEFT IN A CRISP WHITE SHIRT AND TIE AND SMART BLUE TROUSERS. HE IS CARRYING A MATCHING SUIT JACKET.

LENNY: (TO AUDIENCE WHILE POINTING TO SHIRT EXCITEDLY) Mum ironed that last night.

DAD GOES ACROSS TO STAGE RIGHT, HANDS JACKET TO MAM, WATCHES HIMSELF IN IMAGINARY MIRROR

DAD: Lenny!

LENNY: Yes, dad?

DAD: Bring us down the Brylcreem.

LENNY RUSHES OFF AND EXITS STAGE LEFT, WE HEAR HIS HURRIED FOOTSTEPS UP THE STAIRS, THEN DOWN AGAIN. HE RETURNS STAGE LEFT WITH THE BRYLCREEM AND BRUSH IN A LARGE CARDBOARD BOX, RUNS ACROSS STAGE RIGHT

DAD: Ta. You're a good lad, Lenny. (TO MAM) He's a good lad.

MAM: I *know* he's a good lad. Best man in *this* house.

LENNY HOLDS OUT THE BRUSH. DAD TAKES IT. HE BRUSHES HIS HAIR THEN HANDS THE BRUSH BACK TO LENNY. LENNY HOLDS OUT THE BRYLCREEM. DAD UNSCREWS THE TOP, HANDS IT TO LENNY, PUTS HIS FINGERS IN THE GOO AND RUBS IT INTO HIS SCALP.THEN HE HANDS BACK THE BRYLCREEM AND HOLDS OUT HIS HAND. LENNY HANDS HIM THE BRUSH AGAIN. DAD BRUSHES HIS HAIR A SECOND TIME THEN HANDS THE BRUSH BACK TO LENNY WHO IS NOW JUGGLING BRYLCREEM JAR, BRYLCREEM TOP AND HAIR BRUSH CLUMSILY. SUDDENLY HE DROPS ALL THREE.

MAM: (ANNOYED) Be careful of the rug!

DAD BENDS DOWN, PICKS UP THE ITEMS ONE BY ONE, PUTS TOP BACK ON JAR, HANDS EVERYTHING BACK TO LENNY WHO IS NOW JIGGING UP AND DOWN THROUGH NERVOUSNESS.

DAD: It's nowt to fuss over.

MAM: It is for *some*.

DAD: Nowt to fuss over, I said.
DAD TAKES HANDKERCHIEF FROM TROUSER POCKET, WIPES HIS HANDS, PUTS HANDKERCHIEF BACK IN POCKET, STRAIGHTENS HIS TIE, TAKES JACKET FROM MAM AND PUTS IT ON, ALL THE TIME LOOKING IN THE MIRROR

LENNY: (TO AUDIENCE) His hair shone like his shoes.

SUDDENLY DAD PUTS HIS HAND TO HIS NOSE AND PULLS IT AWAY WITH A CRY OF PAIN.

LENNY: (TO AUDIENCE) If there was a long hair in his nose, he always pulled it out.

DAD: Atchooo!!!

DAD TAKES OFF HIS SLIPPERS, PUTS ON HIS SHOES AND LACES THEM. HE AGAIN STUDIES HIMSELF IN THE MIRROR

LENNY: (TO AUDIENCE) But he never looked at his teeth, because they were false, nor at his hands which were black and calloused from the acids he worked with.

DAD: Ow do I look?

MAM: (GRUDGINGLY) You look fine.

SHE SITS ON CHAIR

DAD: What time's dinner?

MAM: Usual time.

DAD: Lenny, I'll bring thee summat back.

LENNY: (EXCITEDLY) Lemonade!

DAD: Lemonade! (HE CHECKS HIS FLIES)

LENNY: (TO AUDIENCE) That was the signal. As soon as he checked his flies, he'd be gone.

DAD: (TO MAM AND LENNY) I'll see you then!

DAD EXITS STAGE RIGHT. MAM AND LENNY WATCH HIM GO. SOUND OF FRONT DOOR OPENING AND SHUTTING. NAN STAGE LEFT TAPS HER WALKING STICK THREE TIMES, PICKS UP SHOEBOX FROM UNDER TABLE, AND MARCHES OVER STAGE RIGHT. SHE SITS DOWN OPPOSITE MAM

LENNY: (TO AUDIENCE) And that was the signal for nan to bring out the photos she kept in the shoebox tied up in bundles with giant rubber bands.

NAN: (TAKING OUT PIX AND LOOKING AT THEM) Oh, I remember those two. Brothers they were, big handsome lads. Well, you can tell. (BEAT) But one died down the pit and the other was killed in an air raid.

LENNY: (TO THE AUDIENCE) She would sift through the photos. Brown men with hollow cheeks, cloth caps and whiskers standing stiffly alongside brown women against brown brick buildings, brown charabancs, brown foliage.

LENNY RUNS TO STAGE RIGHT AND SITS AT NAN'S FEET

MAM: They're too old, those photos. I bet you don't remember half of them.

NAN: Yes, I do…

MAM: I'll stay here a bit and read the paper.

SHE PICKS UP THE REST OF THE SUNDAY PAPER AND GLANCES AT IT. THEN SHE THROWS IT DOWN, GETS UP AND GOES STAGE LEFT, BEGINS TO SET THE TABLE WITH THREE PLATES AND KNIVES AND FORKS

LENNY: (TO AUDIENCE) But as the morning went on, she would have to see to the dinner. Nan and I would be alone.

NAN: (STILL LOOKING THROUGH PHOTOS) This is a lass I used to work with when I was in domestic service. Very pretty woman. Married an Irishman. What was his name? I can't think (BEAT) Oh, they were good times…!

LENNY: (TO AUDIENCE BUT LOOKING AT NAN) I never remembered her talking about anything other than *good* times. (BEAT) And her fondest memories were of one man…

NAN: Your Grandad Guthrie.

LENNY: (TO AUDIENCE) And there he was. Staring out brownly from the brown world.

LENNY GETS UP, RUNS TO BACK OF CHAIR AND PEERS OVER NAN'S SHOULDER

LENNY: He's got a moustache…!

NAN: *All* the men did in those days. Everybody said he looked like Joe Stalin. (BEAT) The spitting image, people used to say.(BEAT) Your Grandad Guthrie was such a man as would walk straight across the road, looking neither right nor left, his hand raised high to warn the traffic he was not to be hindered. Now he *was* a man! You don't see his like these days. Not in *this* house!

LENNY: (INNOCENTLY) Did he never get run over?

NAN: When he travelled on the bus in plain clothes, a ripple of fear would run through the ranks of the criminal classes seated on the top deck. (BEAT) There's a D on the bus, they'd say, D for detective.

LENNY: And for *dabble*. And *daylight*. And *dagger*. And *dim*. And *daffodil*!

NAN: That's right! It's no wonder you do so well at school. You won't be working in a factory when *you* grow up! Not like your dad!

LENNY: (TO AUDIENCE) And *downfall*. D is for *downfall*.

NAN: Your Grandad Guthrie was set to become a chief inspector, very high up in the Sheffield police when fate dealt him a blow.

LENNY: (TO AUDIENCE) D for *dealt him a blow*.

NAN: The Prince of Wales was coming to Victoria Station in his Royal Train. Your

Grandad Guthrie was one of the official party chosen to welcome him. It was a very small party. It was a very big honour. Oh yes.

LENNY: What happened then, nan?

NAN: As if you didn't know!

LENNY: But I still want to hear!

NAN: On the big day, your Grandad Guthrie fell over on the platform, and a senior officer…

LENNY: (ANTICIPATING) …Smelt drink on his breath!

NAN: …Smelt drink on his breath!

LENNY: (TO AUDIENCE) D for *drink*! D for *demotion*! B for *back on the beat*. Rather than accept it, he resigned. He became a private detective.

NAN: He used to follow husbands to hotels…

LENNY: (TO NAN) Why? Were they burglars? (THEN TO AUDIENCE) But the strange hours and the shabbiness were too much for nan. She nagged him to get a regular job. So he became a security guard at a place nan only ever referred to as The Arcade.

NAN: It was a good place, The Arcade. It was a friendly place.

LENNY: (TO AUDIENCE) Especially friendly to a man like Grandad Guthrie. Soon he was eking out his salary with little perks from some of the shopkeepers for whom he was prepared to be exceptionally watchful. But Fate had a *second* blow to deal.

NAN: One day, as he walked past the greengrocer's shop, the street blind fell down, striking him a glancing blow on the right shoulder. (SIGHS) Your Grandad Guthrie marched into the shop to give the owner a good talking to…

LENNY: (TO AUDIENCE) And came out £5 richer! (BEAT) But he'd overreached himself.

NAN: The greengrocer's brother-in-law was an alderman.

LENNY: (PRETENDING SHOCK) An alderman! (THEN TO AUDIENCE) It was here I lost the thread. I didn't know what an alderman was, except it was somebody *very* important. Like next one down from the Queen. But the upshot was Grandad Guthrie went back to following husbands until his sudden death of an undefined internal complaint four years later.

LENNY WALKS TO FRONT OF STAGE

LENNY: (TO AUDIENCE) But his downfall didn't matter. Not to *me*. What made Grandad Guthrie a hero to me was the leftovers from his working life: a set of sepia photographs, most of them faded, all of them numbered, of the same criminal classes who had called out a warning on the bus; a pair of shiny handcuffs that my slender wrists easily evaded; and two truncheons – one standard issue with leather strap, the other a kind of ceremonial version in white wood with blue ribbon. (BEAT) And there had been another souvenir – a revolver.

NAN: A Smith & Wesson 32 calibre. But your Uncle Alfred threw it in the canal. Just before your Grandad died.

LENNY: (RUSHING BACK TO NAN'S SIDE) Why, nan? Why did he do that? (TO AUDIENCE) But nan never answered me. She merely shook her head and…

NAN TAPS HER WALKING STICK THREE TIMES ON THE FLOOR. MAM COMES IN FROM STAGE LEFT

LENNY: That's a shame. About the gun. I Like guns.

MAM: (INTERRUPTING) Guns! I don't know! What's the world coming to? You shouldn't encourage him. You'd think we'd have better things to talk about in this house! You'll give him more nightmares, you will. As if we didn't have enough! (BEAT) Anyway, dinner's ready. (BEAT) Let's put the wireless on. Have a bit of pleasure for once!

NAN AND LENNY TAKE THE THROWS OFF THE CHAIRS, DROP THEM ON THE FLOOR AND CARRY THE CHAIRS ACROSS TO STAGE LEFT. MAM SWITCHES ON THE INVISIBLE RADIO. SOUND OF STATIC THEN *WITH A SONG IN MY HEART* BY THE ANDRE KOSTELANETZ ORCHESTRA.

JEAN METCALFE: (ON THE RADIO) Welcome to another edition of Two-Way Family Favourites. And the first request…

WE HEAR *EVERY TIME WE SAY GOODBYE* BY ELLA FITZGERALD. THE CHARACTERS SIT AT THE TABLE, EAT AN INVISIBLE MEAL AND TALK OVER IT.

NAN: He's got a nerve, that husband of yours. This is a lovely dinner. Lamb and roast potatoes. He's got a nerve not being back to enjoy it.

LENNY: I *love* roast potatoes.

MAM: So does your dad. I made them special.

NAN: Special*ly*!

LENNY: (MIMICKING NAN) Special*ly*! (BEAT) No wonder I do so well at school!

NAN: And rhubarb tart and custard! What more could he want? (BEAT) It'll spoil. If he's not back, if he's not home. It'll spoil. This lovely dinner. This dinner you've worked hard at making. Because he's not back to eat it with us.

JEAN METCALFE: (ON THE RADIO) Now, with belated birthday wishes to Colour Sergeant William Musgrave from all at No 42, Marsden Street, Liverpool , we have Fred Astaire singing Top Hat. Here it is, William, specially for you!

WE HEAR FRED ASTAIRE SINGING TOP HAT. AGAIN THE CHARACTERS TALK OVER IT

LENNY: (LAUGHS) Special*ly*! (PAUSE) I'll never work in a factory, will I, mam? (HE WALKS TO FRONT OF STAGE AND SAYS TO AUDIENCE) When we finished, we stacked the pots in the sink. Mam put dad's dinner back in the oven.

MAM: It'll go hard. All that gravy.

NAN: Hard as a brick. And it was a *lovely* dinner. (PAUSE) Wasting his time. Buying his friends. He just comes swaggering home in his own time, that one. (BEAT) I'll go and look out for him.

NAN AND MAM CARRY THEIR CHAIRS TO STAGE RIGHT AND PUT THE THROWS BACK. MAM RETURNS STAGE LEFT. NAN GAZES OUT STAGE RIGHT, AS THOUGH THROUGH A WINDOW, TAPPING HER WALKING STICK ON THE FLOOR FROM TIME TO TIME

MAM: Lenny, you go in the front room with your nan. I'll bring in the tea.

LENNY: I'll get my comics.

HE RUNS STAGE RIGHT, PICKS UP A PILE OF COMICS FROM BEHIND NAN'S CHAIR AND LIES ON THE FLOOR READING THEM.

LENNY: (TO AUDIENCE) The first comic was Tarzan.

TARZAN VOICE: Ooooaaaooooaaaggghhhhh!!!

LENNY: (TO AUDIENCE) I looked for the end of the story. It said: *Continued next week.* That was no good. You had to have an end to the story. You always have to have an end to your story! I turned to The Lone Ranger and Tonto, his faithful Indian companion. (MOVES ON TO NEW COMIC)

RANGER VOICE: What do you make of these tracks, Tonto?

TONTO VOICE: I think, Kemo Sabay, many men, many horses come this way. Much trouble. Sometimes the tracks are brushed aside with branches from the redwood tree to fool us, yet I see much danger.

RANGER VOICE: Is it not true, Tonto, that, like these tracks, the evil in men's hearts is often hidden? We must always be wary.

FUSILLADE OF GUNSHOTS

RANGER VOICE: Head for cover, Tonto!

LENNY: (TO AUDIENCE) I had a Captain Marvel but I didn't like it much. Billy Batson had been turned into a baby by the evil scientist so he couldn't say *Shazam* and get his super powers back. It came out GOOGOOGOO. I'd read that one before and it was silly. (BEAT) Time passed slowly.

BILLY COTTON VOICE: (SHOUTING) Wakey! Wakey!

WE HEAR OPENING STRAINS OF *SOMEBODY STOLE MY GAL*. AS IT FADES, MAM COMES STAGE RIGHT WITH TRAY AND CUPS

MAM: Here it is. A nice cup of tea. (BEAT) I could do with a cigarette.

NAN: (STILL LOOKING OUT OF WINDOW, SUDDENLY URGENT) Here he is. He's turned the corner.

MAM: (TO NAN) Now, don't start. Don't say anything.

NAN: (MOCKING) *Don't say anything*!

SOUND OF FRONT DOOR OPENING AND SHUTTING. DAD, CARRYING BROWN PAPER CARRIER BAG, ENTERS STAGE RIGHT. HE STAGGERS SLIGHTLY AND HIS SPEECH IS SLURRED

DAD: Ello, 'ello! See what *I've* got then!

LENNY: (GETS TO HIS FEET, EXCITED) Dad! Dad!

DAD: (WAVES BAG) Lemonade! For my Lenny!

MAM: You said you'd be back on time. The gravy's gone solid.

DAD: I don't mind, lass.

MAM: It's spoilt.

DAD: I don't mind, petal.

NAN: It was a *lovely* dinner.

MAM: Take your shirt off so you don't get your food down it. And mind those trousers.

DAD HANDS THE CARRIER BAG TO LENNY, THEN GOES STAGE LEFT, FOLLOWED BY MAM. NAN REMAINS STAGE RIGHT, STILL STANDING BY THE WINDOW. DAD, IN A SLOW UNGAINLY MANNER, TAKES OFF HIS JACKET, TIE AND SHIRT, AND DROPS THEM ON THE FLOOR. HE IS

WEARING A WHITE SLEEVELESS VEST. HE PICKS UP A TOWEL AND TUCKS IT IN HIS TROUSERS. MAM PUTS THE DINNER PLATE ON THE TABLE IN FRONT OF HIM. DAD SITS AT THE TABLE AND BEGINS TO EAT THE DINNER

LENNY: (OPENING THE BAG AND TAKING OUT BOTTLE OF POP) It's not lemonade! It's ice cream soda!

DAD: (GLEEFULLY): All the better! (HE SLURPS HIS FOOD)

LENNY RUSHES ABOUT, SETS BOTTLE ON THE KITCHEN TABLE, TAKES OUT A TUMBLER, POURS INVISIBLE POP INTO THE TUMBLER AND WE HEAR SOUND OF POP FIZZING. DAD, EATING AWAY, PICKS UP THE BOTTLE OF SAUCE

DAD: (TO MAM): Sauce is empty.

MAM: It's a new bottle.

DAD: Not the thick. Not the *brown* sauce. The thin sauce. The *Worcester* Sauce. (GIGGLES)

MAM: It's a new bottle.

DAD: There's nowt left.

MAM: It's a new bottle.

DAD: There's nowt.

MAM: It's a new bottle. Give it a slap.

DAD: (SLAPS BOTTOM OF BOTTLE) Oh yeah. That's right. It's OK Now. (BEAT) I'm partial to a drop of that sauce, *I* am.

MAM: We can all see that!

DAD: Oh. Oh yeah.

DAD POURS WORCESTER SAUCE ON HIS DINNER. LENNY RUNS TO FRONT OF STAGE, BEGINS TO DRINK HIS IMAGINARY POP. DAD WATCHES HIM. THEN LENNY LOOKS BACK AT DAD. DAD WINKS, PICKS UP THE SAUCE BOTTLE AGAIN AND BEGINS TO DRINK FROM IT. THERE IS A SINGLE LOUD GLUG SOUND. DAD PUTS THE BOTTLE DOWN. LENNY BURSTS OUT LAUGHING. DAD PICKS UP THE SAUCE BOTTLE AGAIN AND DRINKS FROM IT A SECOND TIME. TWO MUCH LOUDER GLUG SOUNDS. LENNY BECOMES HYSTERICAL WITH LAUGHTER. DAD PICKS UP THE BOTTLE A THIRD TIME AND DRINKS FROM IT AGAIN. THREE VERY LOUD GLUG SOUNDS.

LENNY: (JUMPING UP AND DOWN, SHOUTING TO AUDIENCE) And he drank the whole bottle! All the Worcester Sauce! Just like it was lemonade. Just like it was Ice Cream Soda. Just like it was Ginger Beer.

DAD: (WIPING HIS MOUTH) Aaaaaaaahhhh!! (HE ALSO LAUGHS HYSTERICALLY)

NAN WALKS TO STAGE LEFT

MAM: (ANGRILY) I suppose you think that's clever in front of the boy!

DAD: (STILL LAUGHING) Just what I needed, flower.

NAN: (ALSO ANGRY BUT MORE MEASURED THAN MAM) It's the drink talking.

MAM: You'll be sick after that.

DAD: (BECOMING ANGRY HIMSELF) What if I am, eh? What if I bloody am?

MAM: It's rhubarb for pudding. (INDICATING SECOND PLATE ON TABLE) Look. The custard's got a skin on it now.

DAD: Don't go wittlin' on about it, lass. I *like* the skin.

DAD STARTS TO EAT THE IMAGINARY RHUBARB TART. THE WOMEN MARCH TO STAGE RIGHT. LENNY GLANCES BACK AT DAD. ONCE STAGE RIGHT, THE WOMEN SIT IN THEIR CHAIRS, MAM PICKS UP THE PAPER, NAN SITS IN SILENCE, STARING AHEAD, TAPPING HER WALKING STICK ON THE FLOOR. LENNY LIES ON THE FLOOR READING HIS COMICS, OCCASIONALLY SIPPING HIS IMAGINARY POP

RADIO VOICE: And that's the end of the Billy Cotton Band Show for another week.

DAD IN THE KITCHEN TURNS OFF THE INVISIBLE RADIO. HE HAS FINISHED HIS RHUBARB TART AND IS NOW SOBERING UP A BIT. AFTER A WHILE HE GETS UP, PICKS UP HIS JACKET, TIE AND SHIRT FROM THE FLOOR AND WALKS SLOWLY TO STAGE RIGHT

DAD: (SUDDENLY APOLOGETIC) I'll wash pots before I go to bed. Lenny can dry.

LENNY: (WITHOUT LOOKING UP) I'm reading me comics.

DAD: (SUDDENLY BELLIGERENT) I said tha can *dry*. What's tha reading? Comics again? I thought thee mam told thee t'read summat decent. (PAUSE) Can't 'e join a library or summat? Read some decent books?

MAM: Leave him alone. *He's* no trouble. I've not seen *you* read a book lately. Only the form book. I suppose you've had a bet.

DAD: (GUILTILY APOLOGETIC AGAIN) A few bob, that's all. (PAUSE) I don't like the lad readin' comics at *his* age. Starts 'em off wrong.

NAN: That's one thing her father never did. That's one thing Grandad Guthrie never did.

DAD: (SARCASTICALLY) Read comics?

NAN: Give his money to bookies.

DAD: (ANGRY AGAIN) It's only bloody thing he *didn't* do from what I kin mek out. I'm sick of hearing about 'im, even if he is her bloody dad!

MAM: Language!

NAN: It's the drink talking, that's all it is. (BEAT) He was a wonderful man was her father. A *real* man. Not like some I could mention. (BEAT) At least he never had to buy his friends with rounds in the pub. At least he wasn't (BEAT) *common*. Oh no, people would look round...

MAM: How much?

DAD: Only coupla bob.

NAN: Good money after bad. It's a mug's game. That's what her father always said.

DAD: Leave 'er bloody father out o' this!

NAN: And he never used language! Not in front of children!

MAM: (VERY UPSET NOW) You never win. You study form week in week out. What good does it do?

NAN: Scum of the earth, that's what he used to call bookies.

DAD: (LOUDER NOW) Never win? What about last Easter then? What about that?

MAM: Last Easter? What about last Easter?

DAD: You bloody know…

NAN: Language! Language!

DAD: You bloody know bloody well! Fifty pounds I med. Fifty pounds on four 'orses!

NAN: Once in a blue moon. A mug's game.

DAD: (VERY LOUD NOW): She allus gets summat when I win. She does! The brown coat! It paid for that!

NAN: She never wears it.

DAD: She doesn't complain *then*. Not then. Oh no, it's a different tale then!

NAN: She never wears it. You never take her anywhere. Never anywhere that isn't common. Where does she get the chance to go that's half decent, where she can wear a decent coat? And what if you *do* win now and again? What's the good of it? That's what her father used to say. He'd got it all weighed up. You win one week, the bookies get it back the next. Of course they do! You're *keepin'* them bookies! Keepin' 'em in style! And you don't see it!

DAD: (FURIOUS) And thee can keep out of it! It's my 'ouse, isn't it? It's my name ont' rent book! (PAUSE, HIS VOICE BECOMES CALMER) Get up, lad. Thee an' me's washin' up. Come on. For tha mam's sake.

MAM: (HER VOICE IS ALSO QUIETER, VERY DELIBERATE) Leave him alone. I'll do it myself. Like I always do.

DAD: Look, there's no need for that. No need. I said I'd do it, didn't I? An' it won't 'urt lad to 'elp!

NAN: (HER VOICE IS LOUD AND TEARFUL NOW) You've never wanted me in this house! I've always known that! I'll not stay where I'm not wanted!

MAM: (VERY CALM) Don't be silly. He doesn't mean it. It's just Sunday afternoon again. (PAUSE) Well, aren't you going to bed now, now that you've done your damage? Sleep it off. It's what you usually do.

DAD LOOKS AT HER FOR A MOMENT THEN HIS HEAD DROPS AND HIS WHOLE BODY SAGS. THE TOWEL FALLS ROUND HIS ANKLES. HE TRIES TO PICK IT UP BUT STUMBLES AND LOSES HIS BALANCE. HE OPENS HIS MOUTH, CLOSES IT, THEN TURNS, WALKS OUT ACROSS TO STAGE LEFT AND EXITS, CRESTFALLEN. WE HEAR HIS FOOTSTEPS GOING UP THE STAIRS IN STUMBLING FASHION. AFTER A MOMENT OR TWO, MAM GOES OVER STAGE LEFT AND LENNY GETS UP AND FOLLOWS HER. THEY BOTH LOOK UPWARD AS THOUGH GAZING UP THE STAIRS

MAM: (SHOUTING) Tea's at six. It's corned beef. See you set the alarm.

MAM WALKS SLOWLY BACK TO STAGE RIGHT AND SITS IN HER CHAIR. LENNY COMES TO FRONT OF STAGE. THE LIGHTS GO DOWN EXCEPT FOR ONE SPOT ON LENNY

LENNY: (TO AUDIENCE) Hear that? (HE CUPS HIS EAR WITH HIS HAND) Silence. (BEAT) No Ella Fitzgerald. No Jean Metcalfe. No bloody Billy Cotton. (PAUSE) The Lone Ranger was right. You have to seek out the tracks of your enemies and pursue them. (PAUSE, THEN SINGS) Mrs Croome flies on a broom but she’s got to come down in the end. (BACK TO SPEAKING VOICE) I decided to seek out the witch and destroy her. I continued to give the front of her house a wide berth, but I began to position myself regularly in the fields at the back, looking out for her, the way my dad looked out for Rommel when he was in the Desert Rats. From my hiding place, I would study her as she filled the kettle from the kitchen tap or dusted the dresser in the back bedroom. (BEAT) Every time I caught her unaware like this, I would stare at her, beam at her my hatred, my concentrated loathing. (BEAT) When I couldn't see her, but I knew she was in the house, I would pour my malice into the brickwork, letting it seep into the walls like damp and lie there. Sometimes I would take out one of my comics. (BEAT) I started with the Tarzan that continued next week. Then I'd take some matches out of our kitchen. (BEAT) I'd tear the pages of the comic into little strips, set them ablaze and let the wind take them, a sacrifice to the savage god of children. (PAUSE) But after a while, rather than use my favourites (HE TICKS THEM OFF ON HIS FINGERS) The Lone Ranger, Roy Rogers, The Ringo Kid - *all complete stories in this issue*! (BEAT) Rather than that, I would take out a few brown pictures that I guessed nan wouldn't really miss. (HE HEADS INTO DARK, RETURNS WITH SHOE BOX, TAKES PHOTOS OUT OF SHOEBOX, TEARS UP A COUPLE) And I'd tear them and I'd burn them. (BEAT) Well, she had so many! (KNEELS DOWN AS THOUGH PRAYING) Go away, witch! I would say to myself, lying in the grass, watching the witch's house. Go away, horrible witch! And I prayed: *Oh God, let her die! She's old anyway. I want her to die.* (PAUSE) And then, one day, she really died!

STAGE LIGHTS GO ON. MAM IS STANDING STAGE RIGHT, DAD IS SITTING AT THE KITCHEN TABLE, READING THE DAILY MIRROR. MAM WALKS ACROSS TO STAGE LEFT

MAM: (TO DAD) That Mrs Croome passed away. Well, she'd just turned 90, so she had to go some time soon.

DAD: All for the best. (QUICKLY) There's a world of difference between 90 and 78.

LENNY: (STILL AT FRONT OF STAGE) Is that how old *nan* is? Seventy-eight?

MAM: (TO LENNY) She's fine. Don't worry. Your nan is fine. Though she's been a bit off-colour of late, a bit confused. She's lost some of her old photos and it's upset her. I expect they'll turn up. In the end.

LENNY: (SUDDENLY WITH UNSEEMLY JOY) I expect nan will die too!

MAM AND DAD TURN AND STARE AT LENNY IN HORROR. STAGE LIGHTS GO OFF LEAVING THEM FROZEN IN SPOTLIGHT. THE SPOT DIMS. NEW SPOT ON LENNY

LENNY: (TO AUDIENCE) They were funny people, my mam and dad. They'd come through a war and it had just made them silly. They'd forgotten what danger was. But *I* knew. I too had been through a war and won. I revelled in my new-found power. (PAUSE) And six months later nan died too. And it's strange now I look back. She *was* like me after all, the one who knew about danger. And she knew I'd work in an office. (PAUSE) And now they're all gone. (BEAT) But *I'm* still here.

HE TURNS, WALKS INTO THE DARKNESS, RETURNS WITH A WALKING STICK

LENNY: There. That's *my* stick. That's *my* stick *now*.

HE TAPS THE STICK THREE TIMES ON THE FLOOR AND GRINS. SUDDENLY WE ONCE AGAIN HEAR FRED ASTAIRE SINGING TOP HAT. LENNY BEGINS DANCING RATHER STIFFLY BUT GETS INTO THE RHYTHM AS HE SASHAYS ROUND THE STAGE AND EXITS GRACEFULLY STAGE LEFT.

LIGHTS DIM
END

About the author

Michael Yates was successively reporter and film critic on the Sheffield Star newspaper, and also worked as a subeditor for the Bradford Telegraph & Argus and the Huddersfield Examiner.

He taught playwriting at Harrogate Theatre and creative writing for the Workers Educational Association, and in 2010 was Writer in Residence in Bradford Schools.

He has had short stories published in magazines and anthologies and won short story prizes from the Jersey Arts Centre, The Armagh Writers Festival, the Wolds Words Festival and The Writers & Artists Yearbook.

Michael has been Poet in Residence in Whitby, in Wakefield Hospitals and at Wakefield Cathedral, and has published three volumes of verse.

A dozen of Michael's plays have been performed in the North of England, including Liverpool, Manchester, Wakefield, Leeds and Bradford, and one of his plays won the Stanley Arnold Trophy at the Sheffield One-Act Play Festival in 2009.

Also by Michael Yates in Nettle Books

The Bronte Boy

Young Branwell Bronte, who once ruled an imaginary world, is now a man, grown mad trying to cope with the *real* one. Having failed as a poet and painter, as doomed in love as he is in literature, he slips ever more quickly down the road of drink, drugs and despair. His loving father Patrick and talented sister Charlotte fight a last-ditch stand for his salvation, but it is Branwell's sinister friend, gravedigger John Brown, who threatens to have the last word in this ultimately terrifying take on the brilliant family we have read so much about and all thought we knew so well. Full text of the play plus cast lists.

Paperback. 80 pages. £6.
ISBN 978-0-9561513-1-5

Life Class

A collection of more than 90 poems about life, love and plenty of other things that don't even alliterate!
"Delight in the careful observations and appreciate the wisdom of the depictions, for reading this book is truly a life class" – John Irving Clarke in his introduction.

Paperback. 112 pages. £9.95.
ISBN 978-0-9561513-0-8

www.ingramcontent.com/pod-product-compliance
Lightning Source LLC
Chambersburg PA
CBHW031844170626
46807CB00004B/1614

9780956151339